Father Dirt

Taylor J. Thompson

PSYOP PRESS

FATHER DIRT

First Edition. February 2025.

Copyright © 2025 Taylor J. Thompson

Print ISBN: 978-1763775404

E-Book ISBN: 978-1763775411

Written by Taylor J. Thompson

Cover Art by Paige Geard (Instagram: @wanderingwitchtattoo)

Father Dirt is written using Australian English. Some words and phrases may be spelt differently than is common.

For the dead.

Chapter One

January 1900

Five years had passed since the slope gave out and the dirt fell, but the body of Matthew Faulds had yet to be exhumed.

Nearly all of the Faulds' outer paddock had been consumed by the landfall. The Pile, as it had grown to be known about the small farming community of Yahl, reached higher than the peaks of the eldest gumtrees that curtained the town. It was a great black blotch against an otherwise picturesque landscape of South Australian countryside.

Mary Faulds, twenty-four years old and five years widowed, stood at the edge of the outer paddock. Her five-year-old daughter Lilith stood beside her, their hands intertwined and The Pile some fifty yards out in front of them.

It had been too long since Mary last paid a visit. The grave was no more than a couple stones throws from the homestead and she often told herself that this should make for regular pilgrimages. It was not right to leave the dead alone for such lengthy periods of time.

For the first years she had made sure to visit every morning and had laid flowers on Sundays after church, but picking at the wound so regularly did little more than ensure it would never heal. She could not wallow in her misery, not with a daughter to raise and a farm to manage. *Self-pity is a luxury reserved for the wealthy,* Mary often thought, *and we have no time for it here.*

Mary was yanked from her daydream and into the paddock by Lilith. "C'mon Mumma," cried out the little girl as she tugged on Mary's arm, urging her along.

The harsh light of a summer afternoon's sun bore down on them as they trudged along. Mosquitos feasted on their ankles, and blowflies clung to their sweat streaked faces like bulbous black boils waiting to burst. Mary did her best to shoo them away, but her daughter seemed unfazed by the pests.

The outer paddock had not been touched since the accident and weeds had long since replaced the crops. They moved through the overgrowth with long arched strides, occasionally stopping to check the ground for snakes or to claw away knots of obstructive vegetation that blocked their path. With each step the dirt pile grew taller.

"Watch your feet," Mary instructed, "Who knows what's living out in this mess."

Lilith mumbled an approving sound. The little girl was dressed in her old feedbag dress that Mary had restitched a few days prior, and her hair was twisted to a tangle as wild as the outback bush. Mary had seen to brushing and ribboning the child's hair twice already, each time it lasted no more than an hour before she would do something to ruin it. In her child's other hand, she held a bouquet of catsear and wildflowers picked from the edges of the veranda. Lilith was shaking with excitement.

Halfway through the thicket the anticipation seemed to become too much for the girl, she broke her grip with Mary and started into a dash for The Pile. Her arms swung back and forth vigorously as they cut through the overgrowth, knocking pieces off her bouquet with each shriek filled stride she took.

Mary followed the discarded petal path left in her daughters wake up to the edge of the dirt. At the base of the mound laid Matthew's memorial carved from limestone, it read; *Matthew Faulds. Husband, Son and Father to be. 1873-1894.* Moss had taken root in several of the letters and dirt coated the top like flakes of ash from an open fire. *I've stayed away too long,* Mary thought.

Lilith crouched down beside the stone and whispered a short prayer that Mary could not quite hear, before laying the handful of weeds atop the carving. "I missed you Father Dirt," said Lilith.

Mary winced at the name. "I'm sure Dad missed you too."

For over four years Mary had kept her daughter's ears clean from the gossip that permeated the town. All her hard work had been undone in an instant last year on the eve of the final harvest, when Faulds Farm's senior hand Big Tom went and drank the public house dry in celebration and woke the whole farm on his return home. He managed to stay conscious just long enough to spill the beans to Lilith about The Pile's origin before stumbling back into the night and passing out in a bush beside the outhouse in a puddle of his own piss.

In the aftermath Lilith had many questions, but Mary had few answers. The child became obsessed with the dirt and against Mary's wishes they started making occasional visits, in short order Lilith decided to rechristen Matthew with a new name, Father Dirt.

It was a crude name, lacking in the dignity and respect that the man himself had held in life. She'd pushed back against the change, but Lilith was adamant and only a fool argues with a five-year-old.

Now that her daughter had paid her respects, she wasted no time in getting to play. Lilith pounced onto the dirt like a barn cat on a magpie and started scurrying up the steep black slope on all fours, kicking up sprouts of dirt behind her that showered Mary and the headstone alike.

"Careful," Mary called out, "I'm not mending that dress again if you tear it."

"I will be Mumma!"

Mary brushed away what debris she could from the memorial. *It's fine, Matthew would have gotten a kick out of this. Children often play with their fathers by riding on their backs, this is not all that dissimilar.*

She watched her daughter's every step until she reached the summit. The Pile was so large and the sun's glare so harsh that the little girl's silhouette was almost lost amongst the crumbling curves of the peak. She followed her child until the strain on her eyes became too much to bear and her vision slunk down to the clumps of loose worm-infested dirt that made up the base.

Mary could not help but think about how close the body of her late husband was to her. Everyone's deceased loved ones were buried, but there was something about Matthew's situation that was deeply unnerving, he was not under the ground; the ground had simply rolled over top of him. Her eyes held on the worms writhing in the dirt and a twinge of unease shot through her stomach. No more than a room's length away from her these pests fed on Matthew's body, picking him clean of his flesh, stripping away the man she had loved until he was nothing but bone.

A lump rose up the back of Mary's throat and for a moment she felt as though she might be sick. Desperate not to lose her afternoon tea all over Matthew's resting place she bounded over the paddock's overgrowth and flung herself against the wire fence of the lower field. Head drooping over a wooden post, she held back her already neatly pinned hair and retched. Over and over she heaved, but nothing came up, only thick clumps of spittle.

Drawing back, she wiped her mouth and the tears that pooled in the corners of her eyes. Some days the visits were good, other days the visits were bad, today was a bad day.

"Lilith!" She shouted from the paddocks edge, "Lilith!"

Her little girl's answer came as soft as a whisper. She was high up and far away, but Mary did not wish to go any closer.

"I'm going to check the farm. I'll be back before it gets too late."

She could not hear much of Lilith's response, only enough to piece together that the child had heard her and was happy enough being left alone.

She stuck to the fence line as she moved up to the paddock's gate, from there she retraced her steps back across the upper paddock to the dirt trail that carved the farm in half. The lane ran the entire length of the property, from the homestead at the top of the hill, all the way down to the front gate. She wandered leisurely up the trail. To her left were a block of four paddocks, three that held the livestock and one where The Pile stood. To her right were two fields of withered corn stalks, brittle and brown from the long summer. Alongside the crops stood the barn where the farmhands slept, a chicken coop, the outhouse, and further up the stables. Beyond that, the trail split into a dust clearing, flanked on either side by a scraggly row of dying weeds and sparsely leafed shrubs. At the far edge of the dustbowl, fronted by a dropping veranda, stood the homestead.

The farmhouse was a small building fashioned of pine with a tin roof that stood two stories tall, facilities and sitting room downstairs and a pair of bedrooms above. It had felt like a fairytale castle when Mary first arrived at Faulds Farm. With Matthew at her side, the rotted peeling wallpaper had appeared as elegant tapestries, the congested dining nook a banquet hall and the water damaged and splintered floorboards as finely polished as a ballroom dance floor. Everything was less magical now and she saw things for what they were, expenses. Mary had managed to keep a roof over her and her daughter's heads, but she was not able to keep that roof clear of leaks.

Mary paced about the farm, tending to various chores to try and occupy her mind and time while she waited for Lilith to tire herself out. Periodically she would look over to The Pile to check on her child, she was usually dancing around at the top, occasionally she would slide down the sides on her rear before climbing back up. Mary was grateful that she had managed to talk Lilith out of wearing her good dress, it was bad enough that any dress need be ruined for something so frivolous.

Waste of good clothing aside, it did bring a smile to Mary's face. Her Lilith had an adventurer's spirit, most definitely inherited from her father. Matthew used to spend many an afternoon summiting the cliffs behind the farm. She would worry every time he set off on a climb and he always attempted to reassure her with the same words, *"Relax wombat, everything works out in the end."*

Mary always thought he'd meet his end during one of his reckless excursions, not from something as routine as mending a fence.

In no time the light started to fade. The sun had sunk down to a thin barn-red line that stretched along the horizon and the distant pine and gumtrees had turned to shadow. Mary started for The Pile. All along the front yard clearing she shouted for Lilith to come down, hoping the child would meet her halfway and she would not have to step foot in that paddock again, but her calls fell on deaf ears.

As she approached the outer gate Lilith was in the middle of some game of her imagination. The little girl was talking to herself in an odd rhythm of mumbles followed by shouts, repeated over and over. Mary was too far away to hear what was being said. The talking continued as she moved across the field until her foot crunched down on a brittle stick and gave her approach away. Lilith's silhouette snapped round to face her, and the talking stopped.

"Come on sweetheart," called Mary, "It's getting too dark."

"I want to stay longer," argued Lilith.

"We can't," said Mary, "George and Tom will be coming in now, I need to dish up tea."

"No!" Cried Lilith, "I want to stay."

"Lilith Faulds, get down here now. Remember what they taught you in Sunday school about obeying your parents?"

"Father Dirt says I can stay," said Lilith, "Father before mother."

Mary felt the anxious tug in her stomach return, "Enough nonsense, your dad can't give orders, come inside."

"Yes, he can, and he says I can stay all night."

"Lilith!" Mary's voice turned to a shout, "Get down here."

The child turned her back and continued playing. "Relax wombat," she said as she walked away, "Everything works out in the end."

The words came in the same tone, with the same rising inflection as Matthew when he used to speak them.

Her vision tunnelled. Her breathing grew ragged. The feeling of the rumble that shook the homestead the day of the slide ran up her spine and the sweat pooling across her forehead turned to ice. Mary had not heard those words since the morning of Matthew's passing.

Against the red glow of the sunset Mary saw flashes of Matthew in Lilith's shadow. Years of memories rushed back in a matter of seconds. Dancing around the kitchen by candlelight. Racing each other through the bush on horseback. Sneaking out to the corn fields at night and making love under the stars. *"Relax wombat,"* she heard Matthew's voice as clear as day.

Her surroundings faded away, along with Lilith and the visions of Matthew, until all that remained were vague shapes and colours. For a moment she thought she might faint where she stood, but with clenched fists managed to keep her footing.

Three deep breaths pulled her back to herself. "Down. Now!"

Lilith protested again, but Mary now met her arguing with action. Stomping forwards, she planted a foot in the loose soil and began to ascend the mound. Her body hunched and her hands ripped into the dirt as she clawed her way up The Pile on all fours like a rabid dog.

Halfway up, her shoes flung free from her feet and tumbled down to the ground. Dust clung to her face as she climbed and falling dirt smacked across her lips, filling her mouth with the bitter taste of churned earth.

Above her Lilith stomped back and forth in a tantrum, shouting objections, and kicking at the topsoil. Endless screamed words cascaded down from the peak, but Mary could only hear two, over and over; *Relax wombat.*

Once she reached the summit Lilith tried to run. Mary lunged toward her. Her bare feet sunk into the dirt, and she fell to her knees. The dirt up top was looser than the rest of the pile, Mary found herself stumbling and falling over herself as she chased after the child. On this uneven ground Lilith was more adept, but the girl could only do so much to prolong the inevitable. There was nowhere to run up here and it was only a matter of time before Mary managed to catch her daughter. She grabbed Lilith by the scruff of her collar and pulled her in close, "Where did you hear that? Who told you that saying?"

Mary saw fear in her little girl's eyes for the first time and for a moment felt as though she may have overreacted.

"He told me," said Lilith, "Father Dirt."

Mary was breathing heavily, and her face burned red as though she was standing over the stove, "Matthew," she panted, "His name was Matthew, and he can't talk. I'm your mother and you will listen to me, where did you hear that?"

Everything fell quiet for a moment; the chaos of catching Lilith had given way to an eerie calm and all that could be heard was the quiet whistle of the evening winds. They stared into each other's eyes, neither looked away, until Lilith finally broke the silence, "It was Father Dirt," the little girl insisted.

Mary's face scrunched up; she could feel the dried patches of dirt breaking in the creases of her skin as her expression changed. She grabbed Lilith by the wrist, "No more dirt pile," she said, "No more outside in general, not for a long time. You'll be spending the rest of summer in your room unless you start telling me the truth."

Hand in hand Mary and her daughter climbed down from The Pile, each step of the way Lilith argued. They were both a mess, but Mary looked the worse for wear. Her face looked as though she had just finished work in a coal mine and her legs were trousered in a thin patchy layer of flaking dirt. There was grime trapped under each of her fingernails, stains covered most of her dress, tears had formed in the fabric under her left arm and down along her ribs.

Mary dragged her little girl across the farm and back up towards the homestead. Lilith spoke at length, but Mary said nothing.

Night had all but set in by the time they reached the front yard clearing. The homestead had turned to shadow, lit only by a small ball of faint yellow light that hung from one of the verandas crossbeams, a lantern. A thin silhouette moved back and forth across the light.

As they got closer, features appeared upon the figure. It was George, the junior farmhand, putting away his tools, gloves, and hat on the racks and shelving by the door. He'd come in for tea.

"What happened?" George called out, "Are you alright Mar'?"

George was a good man. Honest, God fearing, and quite handsome, even with the patchy red streaks of sunburnt skin that grazed his cheeks and brow. Beneath the burns and layers of dust that clung to him, his sharp cheekbones and piercing sapphire eyes shone through and proved more than enough to warrant lovesick stares from the local ladies.

He was the junior hand both in age and time spent at Faulds Farm. He'd only been under Mary's employ for one full season thus far, but the young man had such a range of knowledge and carried himself with such confidence that any outsider would assume him to be in charge over the veteran hand, Big Tom.

"Nothing to worry yourself with," said Mary, "But tea is going to be late, I'll bring it out to the barn."

"Not a problem," said George, "Anything I can do to help?"

"I'll manage on my own. Where's Tom?"

"He's on his way in, shouldn't be long now."

"Can you tell him what I told you?" asked Mary as she stepped up onto the veranda.

George nodded. Mary pulled Lilith up in front of her and ushered the girl inside. Lilith started to protest, "I didn't—"

Mary cut her off with a raised hand and pointed finger towards the stairs, "Room."

Lilith skulked away inside. "Don't want to get on your bad side Mar," George chuckled, "You sure you're alright?"

"Fine, just dealing with a child who thinks she's the parent."

"My Ma used to say it takes a village to raise a son, and a miracle to raise a daughter."

"If only I had her for a mother, mine used to say good children are found at the end of firm hands."

"No one seems to have the right answer," said George, retrieving his lantern and starting off down towards the barn, "I both eagerly await and dread having my own."

"Here's hoping you have more luck than me."

The farmhand laughed and Mary watched as the light slowly faded down the trail. She stepped inside, slamming the door behind her. Alone now, feelings of anger gave way to unease. How did Lilith know Matthew's pet name for her?

When the anxiety would not leave her, Mary decided the best she could do was to get herself cleaned up. *Clean body, clean mind.*

She grabbed two buckets from the pantry and marched out back to the well, filling them as quickly as she could before making her way back inside to the kitchen. From behind drawn curtains she removed her dress and leant over the sink.

With cupped hands she reached into one of the buckets and splashed lukewarm well water over her face and down her body. The water trickled down to the basin, thickened to mud as the layers of grime washed away from her skin. She lathered herself with soap and scrubbed, eager to wash away the dirt and those two haunting words.

Her mind raced trying to think of who could have told Lilith about Matthew's saying, she was the only one he ever spoke it to. The only other person who would have been around back then and may have overheard was Big Tom.

She decided that must be the answer. Tom told Lilith about the saying at some point. If she went out and asked him, he would surely confirm it. The anxiety started to fade at the realization of a logical answer.

She set about preparing a cold supper of ham, buttered rye, cheese, sliced apple wedges and pickled cucumbers for everyone. She placed a plate upstairs outside of Lilith's bedroom, *Mother would have never been this generous,* Mary thought as she set the food down, *perhaps that means I'm doing the right thing.*

When delivering the men's meals to the Barn, Mary had hoped to speak with Big Tom and clear up the incident at The Pile, but by the time she arrived, he had come and gone. Weary of waiting he'd left for the pub.

George offered his sympathies for what had happened and promised he'd clean both plates and see no food went to waste. She thanked him for his kindness, then trudged back inside and straight up to her bedroom.

At the head of the staircase, Lilith's plate still sat outside her door; untouched. Mary cracked the door open; Lilith was sitting on the edge of her bed looking out the window. Her daughter did not turn to face her.

"Flies will take your tea if you leave it out much longer."

Lilith was silent.

"Refusing to eat won't help," sighed Mary, "Make sure you get some, it's a sin to waste food."

Mary eased the door shut and retreated to her bedroom, eager to put an end to a horrible evening. She placed her lantern and the box of matches from her pocket on the bedside table, then dressed herself in her nightgown and climbed into bed.

Darkness had taken hold of Faulds Farm, but the night was still young, and Mary was not tired. She attempted to entertain herself with a book, choosing a recently published novel that George had gifted her a few weeks prior, *The Turn of the Screw* by *Henry James*. She sat propped up in bed. Lantern light flickered across the pages from the nearby table as she started to read.

When it came time to turn the page, she realized nothing she had just read had stuck with her, so she went about reading through the text again. Then again, and again. Mary worked her way through the first page several times yet remembered nothing.

She was too distracted, too upset by the events on the hill. *"Relax wombat,"* the two words loamed large in her mind, there was no space for anything more. *Why would Tom tell her? How would it come up?* The more Mary thought of the incident the less she understood it. *The tone of her voice... She sounded just like him.*

A sting and a flash of heat on the back of her wrist pulled her from the thought. Looking down her skin was torn, red with irritation and blood. In the haze of reliving the moment Mary did not notice herself scratching and picking away her flesh with her fingernails.

She shut the book, placed it by her bedside, and tried for sleep; she would end up waiting some time for it to come. Hours passed and no rest came, only discomfort and restless twisting and turning atop her mattress. Eventually, as the darkness outside deepened and the midnight hour came, she managed to slip into an uneasy sleep.

Rest did not last long. Sleep was but a long blink before Mary's eyes shot back open to the sound of a creaking floorboard.

She jolted halfway up and rested on her elbows. The air that filled the humble room was hot, but Mary sat frozen, ears alert and waiting for another sound to break the uneasy silence. In no time it came; a lingering groan of disturbed wood shifting under the heavy weight of a work boot. The sound was creeping across the ground floor towards the stairs.

The steps came slow but consistent, and with a sense of direction and determination that twisted Mary's stomach into knots. She shifted her weight onto one elbow and leant out over the edge of the bed, her ears perked and listening. The steps were too heavy to be George or Lilith and too light to be Big Tom. A stranger was inside her home.

Mary thought to scream for help, but stopped herself, even if her cries were heard there was no way George or Tom would make it to her before the intruder did. She would need to deal with this herself, or at least make sure Lilith was safely away from danger before calling for the cavalry.

She ripped the bed sheet off her body like a stubborn bandage and flung it to the floor, her feet hit the timber before the bedding had come to a rest. She made for her dresser without a second thought. The hurried thumping of her tiptoed run came in contrast to the drawn-out creaking that climbed the stairs.

Yanking back the handle, the dresser draw came clear off its hinges. A brass key inside rattled against the edges. She gripped the key just as the noise breached the hallway. *Lilith.*

Mary rushed back to her bedside table, jumping down to a slide that sent splinters digging through the skin of her knees. Her hand trembled as she struggled to stuff the key into the lock of the top draw. Sweaty palms and forceful pressing caused the key to slip and bounce off the floor, as the intruder moved into the hallway. The presence of the unseen man was something she had never felt before. Somehow, she knew that whoever it was, was coming for her.

She picked up the key and managed to open the lock. The draw slid open, and Mary pulled out Matthew's old service revolver and a handful of loose bullets. With one hand on the barrel and the other on the grip, she snapped the gun open and started filling the cylinder. Each round that clicked in came with an encroaching step from outside.

With the pistol loaded, Mary got into a firing stance, gun raised and aimed at the centre of the door. Her heart hammered against her chest and breaths came quick and shallow as the presence took the final steps to her bedroom. No matter how hard she tried Mary could not get enough air into her lungs. Sweat streaked down her cheeks like tears. Her hands trembled. She was unsure if she could pull the trigger. Her and Lilith's safety depended on her action, but she could barely hold the gun steady.

C'mon, just like shooting rabbits. She remembered when Matthew used to take her hunting and how he would remind her over and over to control her breathing, *"Through your gut,"* he'd say, *"It'll help you relax."*

Mary focused. Her breathing slowed and a tentative calm came over her. She was ready.

Thud! Thud! Two heavy steps came right up to the bedroom door. Mary waited for a voice. Or a knock. Or for the door to be forced open. But there was nothing. Only silence. Mary cocked the hammer back on the gun, "Who's there?" She called out, "I'm armed!"

No response came. Mary could feel the presence of the intruder out in the hallway, but there was no shadow cast from under the door. No shadow and no lantern light. All that seeped in through the crack was the noxious stench of an open grave.

"Answer me! Who's there?"

Again, her demands were met with silence. Mary felt a tug in the pit of her stomach. It was something akin to a cramp but came with an uneasy nervous feeling. She had a vision of a shadow intruder pausing at her door and after hearing her battle cries, deciding it would be far less trouble to venture down the hall to the unguarded little girl's room. Mary was terrified at the thought. Then, she was angry.

She leapt up and dashed across the room. Flinging the door back she stepped out over the threshold, gun raised and ready to kill. As she moved into the hall, she felt a soft slimy squish beneath her feet that spread out along the sole and oozed up between her toes. Her leg recoiled and kicked in disgust. Small flecks of gunk flung from her foot and splattered against the wall.

In the darkness, the tiny black splotches looked like mould. She ran a finger through one, then brought her hand up close to her face.

"Mud." The word fell from her mouth on a long breath.

Mary looked down at the floor. Boot prints. Muddy ones. There were a series of thick, perfectly shaped prints that came out of the darkness and ended at her bedroom door.

She shook her head, almost as if she were trying to erase the sight from her memory. Mary had mopped up after Tom many times and she had helped George repair his boots in the past, these markings did not belong to either man.

She followed the trail backwards down the hallway towards Lilith's room, the tracks turned at the stairs, avoiding her little girl entirely. Still, Mary cracked the door and peered in. Her finger twitched over the trigger, ready to fire on sight.

Inside everything was as it always was, nothing amiss. Somehow, Lilith was still sleeping, even with all of Mary's shouting.

With her child safe she felt free to pursue the trespasser. She rushed back to her room and grabbed the box of matches from her bedside table. Striking one, she raised the glass on the lantern and touched the flame to the wick. No light. In the chaos of the evening Mary realized she had forgotten to refill the oil; matches would have to do.

She returned to the door and struck a match against the box, an orange burst of flame appeared and dimly lit her surroundings. She held the match low and the pistol high as she followed the muddy prints.

Moving cautiously down the empty hall, she stopped for short moments between steps to listen for any noise. The homestead was silent now, but paranoia filled the darkness beyond her flame with all manner of dangers.

Her head moved on a swivel, waiting for one of the perceived threats to materialize. Between listening for noises and watching the shadows Mary did not notice how quickly her light source was fading. The matchstick crumpled to a charred coil under the weight of the sinking flame. A flash of heat struck her fingertips and her arm jolted outward, releasing the used match into the void. As the sound of the shrivelled stick tapping against the timber hit her ears, so did the sound of the downstairs floorboards creaking.

Mary snapped round to the head of the staircase; pistol raised. "Identify yourself!"

She cocked the hammer back again and waited for a voice to break the silence. When the break came it was not by a voice, but by the returned sound of a groaning floorboard. Fumbling with the gun and matchbox Mary managed to strike a fresh light and made for the stairs.

She followed the ascending muddy boot prints down to the bottom floor. Leaping over the final few steps, she hit the ground with her pistol drawn as the match snuffed out. The homestead was as still as stone as she lit another.

The gun led the way as she stepped forward into the wet squish of the raised prints that emanated from the ajar front door. The grime spread between her toes, but Mary did not kick it away or wince this time. She brushed the mud off against the timbers and continued towards the front door. There was an uneasy quiet as she moved.

She raised the flickering flame up to her face in an attempt to help her see better, the faint whisps of smoke rising from the match caused her eyes to water. Looking about the homestead, she saw nothing.

There were no sounds, apart from the creaking door that swung back and forth in the evening breeze, and nothing was stolen or out of place, save for the boot prints that had come in from outside.

Mary stepped out through the front door, intent on following the tracks further. The boot prints had stained the veranda, but beyond that they were lost in the weeds and dirt of the clearing. The match burnt out on her fingers and Mary was left alone outside in the blind darkness of the country night.

The trail had gone cold, and Mary's anger and adrenaline gave way to reflection. *No prints left the homestead, it's as if whoever broke in, vanished outside my door.*

Chapter Two

At first light Mary marched out of the homestead like a soldier to battle. Down the front yard slope and towards the barn, shouting out to the still stirring farm, "Tom! Get out here right now!"

A muffled echo answered her, "What?"

She searched for the voice; the shriek of a rusted-out hinge saw her find her target. The outhouse door swung open and Big Tom staggered out, his trousers unbuttoned and hanging half off his rear end, one fixed suspender strap all that held them somewhat in place. His shirt was creased and stained with a nights drinking and he was missing both shoes and socks. Even without his work boots he stood half a foot taller than any man in town.

"Morning," the giant called out through a yawn.

Tom was cursed with a permanent crooked eye and a piano key grin of uneven tobacco-stained teeth. Half bald and greyed, he appeared beyond his forty years. A drunk since before Mary met him, but kind too and harder working than any man she had ever known.

She rushed up to him. From behind the big man, the stench of stale beer and pig shit wafted up and hit her like a punch in the mouth. Her face contorted and her eyes welled up. As she fanned the smell away, she looked the giant up and down, lingering on his feet. "Where are your boots?"

The big man scratched at the back of his head and looked away like a scolded schoolboy, "I got some sick on 'em," he mumbled, "Have to clean 'em 'fore I start work. I'll do it ma self though."

"Sick?" Mary asked, "Not dirt or mud?"

"I work in a field," he said, "There's always dirt on ma boots. I cleaned them off pretty good 'fore I walked down the pub though, barman's all uppity as a late. Won't find much mud or dirt, just a little throw up."

Mary let the man's words hang in the air for a moment; *he certainly smells like a man who's been sick on himself.* As best she could tell he was being forth right with her, but still a nagging feeling persisted, and she could not help but think that his missing boots were too coincidental. *Was it Tom who stumbled up to my room? Did he mean to harm me?*

With a deep breath she brushed the festering paranoia aside before it took hold, assuring herself that the shape of the prints did not match the big man's boots. He was far from perfect, but he had always done right by her, and she had no reason to distrust him suddenly after all these years.

After all it was Tom who kept Faulds Farm alive following Matthew's death. While she passed the nights in tears, clutching her husband's pillow, and stroking her belly, wondering what kind of life her child would have without a father, he toiled away in the fields with little more than a reading candle to guide his way. He saved her and never once asked for anything in return.

"Do you ever talk to Lilith about Matthew?" Mary asked.

"Not really, I mostly just listen to 'er. Usually just goes on about the games she plays with 'im up in the dirt, kiddie stuff ya know."

"You haven't told her any stories then? Never mentioned old sayings of his, pet names he'd use?"

"Not that I remember."

"And you haven't got a second pair of boots you never told me about?"

"I feel like I've been nabbed," Tom chuckled, "All these questions, what's gotten into ya?"

"Nothing," Mary insisted, "I just need to know if you have another pair of boots."

"Two pair? I ain't Rockefeller. I really gotta get gettin', heat's causing all sorta problems round here. Promise I'll have the boots sorted 'fore I bring 'em anywhere near the house."

"Of course," Mary nodded, trying to hide her disappointment at the lack of answers, "Thank you, stay safe in the heat."

With a smile and a nod, the big man set off down the trail, back towards the barn. Mary watched a moment, unsure whether his assurances could be believed. *He's a man of many flaws, but deceit isn't one of them, he lacks the cunning for it. Still, when a man drinks enough to euthanize a dog on the daily, can he even trust his own recollections?*

By the time he reached the barn she'd decided he must have told Lilith about the pet name and simply drank the memory away. *The dead don't speak,* she reminded herself, *this is the only rational explanation.* Relief came with the realization, and she told herself that an answer for the muddy boot prints would soon follow. A thieving swagman most likely, she'd have George take word to Constable Dunne about the incident and Lilith would be confined to the homestead as punishment for yesterday, so she would be easy to keep tabs on.

After breakfast she called upon George. He was in the stables, reshoeing Spirit, Matthew's old horse. She told him about the incident in the night, sparing no detail. "I can stay downstairs tonight," he told her, "Keep watch, any man crosses the threshold again and I'll unleash the wrath of God upon him."

"That's kind of you, but I have plenty wrath of my own," said Mary, thinking to the loaded revolver beside her bed. "I'm sure there's no need for worry, still a chance Tom just lost his way, but I thought it best the law be made aware, just in case."

"I'll pass the word on. He got in well past last call, so you're probably right. Either way, no trespasser's getting close to you again, not if I can help it."

Mary thanked the farmhand and returned to the homestead, to her chores.

As dusk settled in on Faulds Farm Mary stood out on the veranda ringing the meal bell. In short order the farmhands emerged from the shrivelled corn crops and started up the trail to the homestead, their faces sweaty and covered in dust from a hard day's work. "Hurry along!" Mary cried out, "I've made a special tea to make up for last night."

"Everything you cook tastes special," called George.

"No one likes a kiss ass," yelled Big Tom.

Mary smirked to herself, "Except for the person getting kissed."

Slipping back inside, she finished dishing up plates. Tonight's meal was a rabbit pie stuffed to the brim with celery, carrot, onion, and potato, with sides of buttered bread, crisp green beans, and boiled corncobs. By the time she'd finished serving, the men were washed and ready to eat, but there was no sign of Lilith. The hands had made their way across the farm, and her girl hadn't managed the stairs. "Lilith," Mary called out from the bottom banister, "Didn't you hear the bell? Teatime."

Returning to the table, she took her seat alongside George and Tom. The three waited patiently but heard no rustling from upstairs. "I said teatime!"

A moment passed in silence, save for the sound of Big Tom's knife and fork impatiently clinking against his plate. George rose from his chair, "Is she alright?"

The farmhand's words gave her doubts. Nothing good came from a child being so quiet for so long.

"She's fine," said Mary, trying her best to assure the men as much as herself, "Just being a little devil. You two sit and eat, I'll see to her."

"You are on thin ice young lady," warned Mary as she rounded the top of the staircase.

She clasped the handle to her little girl's room and ripped the door open; there was no one inside.

Mary screamed her daughter's name, her words came now with a strain of panic instead of frustration. She ripped the blankets off the bed and tore open the wardrobe. There were few hiding spots in the room and Mary checked them all. Nothing but dust mites.

Downstairs the farmhands began calling for her, their shouts echoed out alongside heavy footfall that climbed the staircase. As she began to pick at the back of her wrist, the men burst into the room. "What's 'appened?" Asked Tom, still chewing on a mouthful of rabbit pie.

"Is Lilith alright?" Added George.

Mary struggled for words, all she could think to do was shout for Lilith over and over. When she managed to speak, the words came slow and few, "She's gone... I just checked on her."

George placed a hand on her shoulder, "It's alright, we'll find her, I used to hide from my Pa all the time, it's what weans do. Check the bedrooms, me and Tom will look downstairs, she can't have gone far."

They spread out through the homestead; Mary turned both rooms over from top to bottom. All three called for Lilith, but no one got a response. There was no sign of her daughter anywhere.

With her search exhausted Mary moved to rejoin the others. Stepping down from the bottom step, she noticed a splotch of dried mud beside the skirtings, the sight brought back the uneasy feelings from the night before. The passage of the day had dulled her fears and given her ample time to explain the unexplainable away. Ideas of a drunk and forgetful Tom or a vengeful practical joke from Lilith had all seemed so plausible in the daylight, but now that the windows drew grey with the encroaching darkness and her daughter was nowhere to be found, the fear returned to her tenfold.

"The intruder!" She shouted.

Both men rushed to her with looks of concern on their faces, "The one I spoke about this morning," Mary continued, "From last night, what if they've come back, what if they've snatched Lilith?"

"It's possible," said George, "Dear Lord I hope you're wrong, but it is possible."

The farmhand did his best to appear calm, but in his eyes, Mary saw the same fear she felt. Big Tom put on no such airs. "Bloody bastard!" The giant clenched his fists and for a moment she thought he was going to punch a hole through her wall, "I'll knock this bugger's teeth out when I get a hold of 'im!"

"If someone's grabbed her, we need to move fast," said George.

Upon the realization that her daughter's life might be at stake Mary knew she had to step up. A deep breath brought calm, then action. "George," she said, "Light some lanterns, we'll search the farm. Tom, fetch our freshest horse and round up a search posse. When we find Lilith, I'll join you in knocking his teeth out."

Mary and Tom rushed out to the veranda and slid on their boots; George was close behind. The sky was a deep purple stained with blotched stars as pale as tallow. Precious little light remained, soon the blind darkness of the country night would take hold and the hopes of finding Lilith would be slim to none.

George stepped outside with three lit lanterns in hand. The giant snatched one and without a word broke into a sprint for the stables. Mary had never seen the big man move so fast.

"We should move down the slope," said George as he handed Mary her lantern, "Clear the farm from top to bottom."

"As long as we move fast."

They raised their lanterns high and called for Lilith as they crossed the dirt clearing.

"Structures, then fields," said Mary, hurrying her pace towards the outhouse and chicken coop.

The hinges on the outhouse door squealed as she peeled it open, sending the nearby chooks into a frenzy of startled clucking. Inside, she found nothing but a bad smell.

She slammed the door shut. The sound of galloping hoofs drew her attention up the slope. Through a cloud of dust Big Tom descended on horseback, "Stables are clear," he called from atop the mare as he cut a circle around them, "I'll keep eyes on the road, we'll 'ave the bastard 'fore the hours up, promise."

"Thank you," Mary shouted, "Ride safe, ride fast."

The words had barely left her lips before the giant took off into the night. *To think I doubted him. He'd do anything for us, especially Lilith.*

Mary and George continued the search. George poked around the coop but there were only chickens to be found. Side by side they ran down to the large, chipped red doors of the barn, they moved fast but the encroaching darkness moved faster. "I'll check the perimeter," said Mary, "You check inside, we have to move quicker."

"Shout if you find anything," said Geroge, "And be careful Mar'."

"You too."

George disappeared inside the barn and Mary was alone.

Casting the light from the lantern out in front of her, she started to trace her way along the barn's perimeter. Weeds as tall as sheep dogs littered the structure's edges, the harsh summer had done little to kill them off. Keeping her head low she moved through the brush, raising it sparingly to search. With each step Mary watched as her foot disappeared into the tangled mass beneath, unsure when or if it would hit solid ground.

The glow of the lantern cast silhouettes against the barn wall, turning the overgrowth's shadows into monsters. Every few paces saw her jolt as her mind was tricked into thinking danger approached.

The sky was turning an inky black and little could be seen beyond the lanterns reach. Left alone with nothing but a fist and a lantern to defend herself, Mary's mind went to Matthew's pistol in the bedroom draw. Before now there had been no time to think of anything but Lilith and the intruder, no time to worry about her own safety. She had only thought of finding them, not of what would happen once she did. *A lantern is no gun, but fire and shattered glass are not without stopping power.*

As she approached the rear of the barn, the uneasy sensation that she was not alone came over her. She rounded the corner. A rustling in the weeds drew her eyes. She whipped the light around.

From out the undergrowth skittered a pair of rats, they scurried across her path and leapt into a nearby prickle bush. Mary jumped and let out a squeal, much to her own embarrassment.

"Bastards," The word slipped from her lips.

She trudged on round the bend. There beneath the thicket she spied a pair of glowing red beads. She moved the light across it. As the flicker of the flame brushed over the weed patch, more and more pairs revealed themselves, all lined up, side by side like soldiers standing at attention.

Mary counted nine sets that shone as bright as lost embers. Stepping closer, the lantern gave shape to the blotchy shadows that surrounded them, they were eyes, rat's eyes.

Nine plump rats covered in mud matted fur standing hip to hip, glaring up at her. She thought to herself that such a sight should elicit fear, but rather she was stunned by the improbability of what she was seeing.

Rats could not scare her; they hadn't caused her worry since she was a girl. She remembered the harsh winter back in eighty-four when her father walked out into the pines with an old axe handle and clubbed a quarter pillowcase worth of the rodents to death. It was the first meal she'd eaten in over a week and all she'd eat for the next fortnight. *It's hard to be frightened of something once you've skinned and ate it.*

There was no fear, but rather a festering anxiousness. Why were they watching? Why were they waiting?

She started to slowly back away. The rat's eyes did not follow her. They stayed staring forward, looking right past her. She followed their eyeline and her gut dropped. They were watching The Pile.

Atop the dirt, the silhouette of a thin man wearing a wide brimmed sunhat stood black against a low hanging moon. Mary could see little more than the shape of him, but knew the man was watching her as well.

She felt sick at the sight. Her mind grew fuzzy, and her legs unsteady. In that moment she could have fainted if she allowed herself, but she refused to be as useless as she had been the morning Matthew passed and forced herself to stand her ground. *He took Lilith, I'll not lose more family without a fight.*

"George!" Her voice came with a dry rasp and the line of rats scattered at the shout. She kicked off her boots and broke into a sprint, "George, hurry!"

With burning lungs and blistering feet, she rushed towards the shadow man, all while shouting over and over for George. Her eyes never left the stranger, but the distant creak of the barn door and the sound of George calling to her through strained breath let her know he was not far behind.

In an instant, the dread routinely brought on by The Pile dissipated. Her daughter had been stolen, her husband's grave disrespected, she cared only for justice.

Approaching the upper paddock her pace did not slow. She leapt up, hit the gate, and tumbled over top like a cowboy fleeing an incensed bull. Her lantern smashed against the wood as she flipped, sending shards of glass down into the shadow grass below. As her feet hit the ground a sharp burst of heat tore up along the meaty outer edge of her right foot. Several shards dug into her, and blood began to flow.

With each hard-fought step she felt jagged pieces tug at her foot, unbuttoning her flesh more and more with every stride. Her skin burned red hot, and the blood ran ice cold. She felt as though her foot might give out under the weight of her at any moment, but Mary refused to stop or slow. Above the shadow man remained as still and watchful as a scarecrow. None of the man's features could be made out, but Mary imagined him smirking in amusement at her pain. *He'll suffer more than me.*

She hobbled to the outer gate, swung up a leg and tumbled over top into the paddock. As her feet slammed down into the tangle of overgrown crabgrass, she felt the glass dig deeper into her. Biting her tongue was all that stopped her from yelping. Tears rose in the corners of her eyes, but she did not allow them to fall, no weakness could be shown in front of the shadow man.

She shook off the pain that was climbing up her rapidly numbing foot and looked up at the intruder looming over Faulds Farm, "Bastard!" She shouted, "If you've hurt her, I'll kill you!"

She tore her way through the weeds, as the shadow above started to change. The silhouette of the gaunt man shifted, shrinking smaller and smaller with each step until it resembled a familiar little girl, Lilith.

Her fevered approach dropped to a plodding limp at the sight of the change. Hunched over and desperate for air she stood at the dirt's edge with squinted eyes, unsure how she could have made such a mistake. Her girl was shrouded in darkness atop the peak, moonlight shone just bright enough to give the curled frizz of her hair it's shape and a dull imitation of its colour. She was standing still, murmuring quietly to herself. Mary listened for what she was saying but none of the words were clear.

"Lilith!" Mary shouted, "Get down here right now."

There was no response, not even a flinch at her yelling. Lilith remained motionless, almost as if stuck in a trance.

"Mar'!"

Mary glanced over her shoulder to see George rushing across the outer paddock towards her. Further behind the farmhand, at the bottom of the slope, she noticed a small mass of some half a dozen lanterns funnelling in through the front gate. Tom had gathered the search posse. *An audience for my parental humiliation, how lovely.*

"It's alright George," said Mary as she rolled up the sleeves of her dress and refastened her hair into a tighter bun, "It's like you said, she's just ran away to play kiddie games."

The young man saddled up beside her and raised his lantern, the dull light caught her daughter's eyes, and they shone a sickly silver. They were glassed over and bulging like a bugs, staring out across the farm, seemingly oblivious to her and Geroge, and the group snaking up the trail towards them.

"Want me to go up and get her?" George asked.

"Thank you," said Mary, "But I'm her mother, this falls on me."

"Nothing wrong with asking for help Mar," said George.

The adrenaline was fading, and the pain of her sliced foot was settling in. "You can help with a 'kerchief," she said.

The farmhand reached into a pocket and produced a neatly folded hanky. Mary took it and used it to tourniquet her injured foot. Blood soaked through the fabric in an instant, but with any luck it would be enough to keep dirt out of the wound.

"Good Lord Mar," said George, "You shouldn't even be standing on that."

"I've had worse," Mary assured him, "No need for worry."

She stepped to The Pile. As her first foot sank into the cool soil, she caught a glimpse of her dress and for a moment regretted turning down George's offer, this would be two dresses ruined in as many days.

She raised her injured foot and started climbing as gracefully as she could manage, hopeful that George would not see her in too unflattering a state.

"Go stop Tom," Mary called back as she moved up the dirt, "I don't want spectators for this."

"On it!"

Each step up was hard fought. She'd lost nearly all feeling in her right foot, and it disobediently slipped out from under her when she put weight on it. Dust filled her lungs and stuck to her skin. Mosquitos nipped at her arms and legs, and flies hovered about her like she was a puddle of spilt milk. Still, she pushed on and managed to scale The Pile, though at a much slower pace than yesterday.

As she dragged herself up over the summit, Lilith's murmurs became clear to her, "Not much time, tell them, warn them, now, now, now."

On shaky legs Mary moved towards her daughter, the young girl's eyes fluttered for a moment then fixed on Mary, "Mumma!" She smiled.

Lilith was even more of a mess than usual. Her face was smeared with streaks of dirt that ran down her forehead and over her flushed cheeks. Her hair was visibly knotty and sticking out in all directions, with clumps of crumbling dirt flattened into the hair around her ears. Her dress completely ruined as well, riddled with holes and stains too numerous to count.

"I have to tell—" Lilith started to speak.

"You were confined to the house," snapped Mary, "I thought you'd been kidnapped, or killed!"

When she was done speaking there was quiet. Mary looked down into her daughter's tiny face and remembered she was talking to a child; this anger was too much for such a small soul. She did not like the bitter parent she felt herself being these past two days. Back when her and Matthew found out she was pregnant she had vowed to be a better mother than those that came before her, she was failing to live up to that promise.

"I'm sorry," said Mary, "You scared me. I didn't know where you were or what had happened to you. You know I told you not to come up here anymore."

"I just wanted—"

Lilith was interrupted again, this time from a voice below, "Stop, stop," George called out, "Thank you but we don't need your help after all."

Mary looked down to see a group of eight congregating around the base of The Pile, their bodies were hidden in the darkness, but their faces could be seen peering up through the flicker of lantern light. There was Big Tom at the front along with George who was trying to corral everyone out of the paddock. Behind the farmhands was old man Byrne, dull Mister Arthur and the ever-cheery Williams couple Edward and Alice. Further back the lean Constable Dunne watched in amusement, with a small smirk poking out from under his bushy walrus moustache. Beside him was the one person Mary hoped would not come, the elderly town gossip Miss Mackenzie.

Mackenzie was a woman cursed with a homely face and an even homelier personality. Never married and never any serious prospects, though not for a lack of trying. The spinster had an unquenchable thirst for gossip and a frustrating habit of forcing herself into the centre of any situation. Back when they had laid Matthew's memorial stone, she was the one who everyone sought to comfort thanks to her endless stories about how she looked out for Matthew as a boy and how she knew him better than anyone left in the world.

It came as no surprise when she was the first to call out from the crowd. "Is everything alright dear?"

"Ya need me to come up 'n help?" Shouted Big Tom.

"We're fine," Mary called back, "You can all go, sorry to disturb your evenings."

"No, no dear," insisted the spinster, "We'll wait and make sure you get down okay."

Mary felt her shoulder's tense up and it took all her will power to not let out a curse. She ran her hands up the sides of her face and reaffixed her hair behind her ears, "Alright," she said, turning back to Lilith, "Hurry up, if we get down quick, we might be able to avoid a cuppa with Mackenzie."

"I can't," said Lilith, "I have to talk to Father Dirt again, he said there's a storm coming."

"It's the middle of summer, there's been nothing but sun for months now, there's no storm sweetheart."

"But Father Dirt said so."

"Enough about Father Dirt," said Mary, "I was wrong to snap at you, but that doesn't mean you aren't in trouble young lady. I told you to stop it with this nonsense."

"He told me to honour and obey father," said Lilith, "That's in the bible."

"Matthew was your father; Father Dirt is imaginary, a made-up friend, that's all."

Mary felt herself growing agitated, her cut foot throbbed, her daughter refused to obey her, and her neighbours whispered about her down below. "I'm the only parent you have left, and I said we're going back inside, right now."

"No!" Shouted Lilith.

The girl ran and Mary gave chase. She stumbled after her daughter, slipping in the loose dirt and falling to her knees over and over just as she had the night before, only this time her efforts were cheered on by laughing spectators from the ground. *What monsters laugh at a man's grave? She's turned the three of us into a spectacle.*

Mary spread out into a wide stance and with some fast shuffling managed to corner Lilith. She leapt after her and just barely grabbed the girl by the leg before her face smacked into the topsoil. Her cheeks were caked with dirt and her nose and mouth filled with the bitter stuff. The crowd below broke into offbeat applause and hollering, and Tom let out a high-pitched whistle.

Mary imagined just how dishevelled she must've looked and how poorly all those watching below must've thought of her mothering. She dragged her kicking daughter down The Pile and through the waiting crowd. George rushed up to her side, "You alright?" He asked.

"We're fine."

She might have told him the truth if it were only the two of them, but too many eyes were on her and she felt that if she stopped moving or let too many words slip, she may breakdown, either in tears or screams.

Big Tom gave her a pat on the back as she limped past. The constable smiled and shook his head at her, "No wonder you've got mud all over your floors," he said.

"Mary dear," said Miss Mackenzie, "You should let me take Lilith while you clean this mess up."

"No thank you," said Mary, as she continued towards the paddock gate, "I have it under control, you can leave."

As they neared the fence Lilith dropped her weight and fell to the ground. Mary managed to drag her a couple more feet before it became too much of a strain. "Get up," she ordered.

"No," screamed Lilith as she dug her heels into the weeds, "I have to talk to Father Dirt, there's a storm coming!"

The child's declaration raised the curiosity of those gathered even further. Big Tom rushed up to her side, "What'd she say?"

"Something about a storm," said the spinster, hot on Tom's tails, "And a Father Dirt?"

"That's Matthew," said Tom.

"How's she supposed to talk to him?" chuckled Constable Dunne.

Mary pulled on Lilith's arm, "She doesn't."

"I do," insisted Lilith, "Father Dirt says to me when I come and visit, he says there's a storm and no one is safe."

"There's been barely a cloud all day," called George from the back of the group.

His words caused everyone to gaze up at the night sky. "We should all listen to Mar'," George continued, "Leave them be, this is clearly just a child's imagination gone too far."

They all started debating amongst themselves, everyone spoke at once and drowned out each other's voices. With her neighbours distracted Mary decided to make a move. She reached down past kicking feet, wrapped Lilith up in her arms and hoisted her onto her shoulder, "She's making up stories," said Mary, "Forget her, go home to your tea and rest."

Ignoring the pain in her foot she broke into a sprint, moving hot footed across the grass and up to the homestead. From the veranda she saw a smattering of lanterns and shadowed neighbours disperse in all directions and slowly fade away into the summer's night. *What stories will they tell come morning?*

Inside Mary carried Lilith to the kitchen basin. She disposed of the girl's dirty clothes and scrubbed her as clean as she could with the little water there was on hand. Once clean enough to not ruin the sheets she sent the child to bed.

Lilith let out a few tears and a sniffle as she skulked away and for a moment Mary felt guilty about being so harsh. The guilt did not last long, when she called out to wish Lilith a good night the child retorted that she was stupid for not allowing her to go back to The Pile and claimed Father Dirt would see to her. Mary ignored the comments. *Children are fickle, a few biscuits and a glass of cordial in the morning and she'll be right as rain.*

The whole evening came with a sense of déjà vu. Mary prepared and delivered plates to everyone, then on her way back up to the house she again fetched two pails of water to clean herself.

She was desperate to wash the dirt and evening off, but first her foot would need to be dealt with. She raised her leg up over the basin, dried blood reached across her foot and up her ankle like a rash, it itched the same as one too. She was off her feet and the burden of supporting her weight gone, but somehow this only made the pain sharper.

As gently as she could she wiped away the crusted layers of blood and dirt that clung to her, then with a pair of pliers started to remove the glass. When they failed to reach deep enough into the meat, she sought the assistance of a carving knife. Each piece pulled came with a sting of heat and a gush of fresh blood. When all was done, she counted thirteen shards, a number she found strangely fitting.

A pot of whiskey was put to the boil to sterilize the wound. She twitched and recoiled as the burning liquid filled the cut and dripped down between her toes. *Stop it,* she told herself, *better this than the bone saw.*

She bandaged herself up as best she could, then finished washing and ate a quick supper alone by the light of a weary candle.

Upstairs she collapsed down onto her bed. Her body was tired, but the stresses of the evening kept her tossing and turning for hours before sleep finally took hold.

She dreamt a familiar dream, of her and Matthew standing out in an overgrown lavender field that stretched endlessly in all directions. The gentle sound of an unseen pianoforte filled the air, along with the soft buzzing of thousands of docile bumblebees that hummed along to the tune.

Mary wore a pristine white dress, fashioned out of the finest silks, embroidered with pearls. The sensation of the smooth and delicate fabric rubbing against her skin filled her with an electricity she had not felt since Matthew passed. Her nails were manicured, her hair neatly styled, and her body had been sprayed with an array of perfumes scented with violet, honey, and musk.

Matthew was standing some thirty yards away, dressed in the same suit he had worn on their wedding day. He was just as handsome now as he had been all those years ago.

Mary moved towards him, and he towards her, until they came together in a tight embrace. He smelt of fresh cut hay, a familiar scent but one that never smelt as nice as it did on Matthew. She nuzzled into him and ran her fingers up along the muscular ridges of his back, tracing the familiar path she had once felt so regularly.

Soon they were compelled to motion by the music, the couple settled into a slow dance and Mary instinctually rested her head against Matthew's chest. Song after song they swayed and spun through the untamed lavender bushes, smiles etched on both their faces.

As one song faded into another, Matthew rested a hand under her chin and gently raised her head up from his chest. With his eyes closed and lips puckered he leaned down; Mary rose to her tiptoes and the couple came together in a passionate kiss.

It was a perfect moment. A moment routinely prayed for and always cherished. The kiss was everything she remembered, everything she missed; then suddenly it wasn't.

Mary felt something push past her lips and into her mouth and tickle the backs of her teeth. For a moment she thought it was Matthew's tongue, but as it probed deeper, she realized she was mistaken. It was too thin and oddly shaped; and twisted about in ways that were unnatural for a tongue.

She slipped away from her husband. Her eyes opened slowly at first, then all at once.

Poking through a cavity in Matthew's bottom lip was the slithering body of a gargantuan earthworm. Slimy and coated in a spattering of dirt. All the air left her lungs on a single gasp. Her chest and stomach tightened, it felt as though she had been stuffed into a corset three sizes too small. She wanted to scream but could not so much as catch a breath.

Matthew started to change. The face of her handsome young husband vanished and was replaced by a twisted and decayed caricature.

His skin, yellow and splotchy. His clothes, tattered. Dirt, all over.

His body was frail. Flesh and fat fell from his bones in chunks, exposing portions of skeleton as clean and white as chalk. His handsome face was almost unrecognizable. Booklice scurried in and out of his nostrils and eye sockets. Maggots danced beneath his flesh, pulling the muscle and contorting his rotting face into unnatural expressions of delight. A crooked smile stretched across his face and his shrunken, pus-coloured eyes stared at her knowingly.

Mary stumbled backwards, her mouth agape, desperate for air that would not come. A cold chill bit at her legs. Looking down she saw several mud stains had appeared along the hem of her dress, more quickly followed. The flawless fabric was consumed in seconds. Then the mud spread from the dress to her skin.

Mary scratched and clawed, trying in vain to rid herself of the mud. Matthew stood and watched; the maggot enforced smile still on his face. "I miss my wife," he said, "I want her back."

He lunged toward her. She raised her hands. Darkness consumed her and Mary let out a breathless scream.

Her body jolted and she was sitting upright, back in bed. Her hands clutched the sheets and cold beads of sweat ran down her face. Moonlight poured in through the half-opened windows, bathing the room in soft light and casting twisted shadows against the far wall.

Mary inhaled deeply and rapidly as she looked about the room. Nothing was out of place. No dirt stains. No muddy boot prints. Everything was as she left it.

Relieved she sunk back into her pillow. Trying to find her sleep once more, she heard a faint rumbling in the distance, a thunderclap.

Chapter Three

For Mary Faulds the night passed slowly and without rest. Nightmares and motherhood stresses kept her awake most of the evening, it was not until the witching hour had come and gone that she managed to slip back into an uneasy sleep. It would not last long.

The mocking cackle of a lightning bolt jolted her from her slumber. Yellow light filled the bedroom for a heartbeat, then it was gone. It was as bright and fleeting as the explosions of flash powder that went off when sitting for a photograph. A tired groan was all that separated the strike from the thunderclap.

She threw back the covers and staggered towards the window. The room was cold and dreary. A shiver gripped her, and her arms and legs broke out in gooseflesh. Each step bore a painful reminder of the broken glass in the field. Overnight her right foot had swollen to twice its normal size and the skin about the wound had turned a dark lifeless purple. The colour reminded her of her mother's lips the last time she'd seen her; laid out in a cheap pine casket under drab church lighting.

As she approached the window, the wind outside rose to a shriek. She pressed her palms up against the glass, a thick cloud of condensation gathered in front of her face in an instant. *Lilith guessed right, a summer storm.*

The farm was bathed in dull grey light and walls of wind-swept rain crashed against The Pile. The dirt appeared as a tall pyramid, smoothed by the water, sleek and black like molasses. The fields were flooded, debris blocked the trails and laneways, and hefty branches crashed down from every tree, hitting the soaked grass with bangs like shotgun blasts.

She stared out at the chaos, her lips trembling, "How?" She whispered.

There had been summer storms before, but they were rare and never so severe or accompanied by such a decline in temperature. She wondered how Lilith could have predicted such an unlikely event. Twelve hours ago, she had been outside dragging her daughter down from the dirt on one of the hottest nights of an already blistering season and now she was struggling to keep herself from shaking with the cold. Mary closed her eyes and prayed that Lilith would only be half right, that the storm would not be as destructive as she claimed. The scene outside gave her little confidence.

Her prayer was cut short by a pounding at the front door. It was violent and almost rhythmic. Mary moved for the bedside table; she grasped the top draw handle as a shout from downstairs stopped her. "Mar'?" It was George's voice fighting against the storm, "Let us in!"

She rushed to the call, wrapping herself in her dressing gown as she hobbled down the hall. Lilith was waiting at the top of the staircase, jumping up and down cheering, "The storm! The storm! Father Dirt was right!"

"Back to bed," Mary ordered as she moved around her and down the stairs, "I'll be up in a minute."

She flung the front door open, and a flurry of frosted air rushed in, sending her dressing gown billowing out behind her. Bracing the door with her hip, she fought to wrap the gown back around her body.

In the doorway George and Big Tom stood sopping wet from head to toe. George's hair was clumped together in damp tufts that hung over his forehead and partially curtained his glowing eyes. His soaked through shirt clung to his heaving chest and a beat-up brown jacket enveloped his body. In his hands he held a small pile of pillows and blankets. Big Tom was a step behind him. His clothes dripped like a well pump and his hands nursed a crate of beer bottles.

The men rushed in as if carried by the breeze. Across the farm it appeared as though the rapture had come, and Mary found herself unexplainably drawn to it. Barefoot she walked out onto the veranda. Rain lashed against her, stinging her face and wound. The wind tugged at her robe, nearly ripping it off her body, but still she moved forward.

Out in the fields there was a rustling, the weeds of the outer paddock shook, but not with the wind. A crash of thunder. A flash of light. Black fur and bloody eyes. Amongst the overgrowth a stream of rats moved as if possessed, oblivious to the carnage around them. They raced in a circle around The Pile. Round and round, a black blur.

From the skies a swirl of black and white descended onto the dirt with a chorus of caws that rivelled the rumble of the storm. It was a flock of magpies, too many to count, perched all along The Pile. Their feathers waterlogged and raised, but none seemed to care. Their eyes a muddy red that shone like beacons through the rainy mist.

They squawked to one another and pecked the dirt for grubs and worms. Shaking, Mary stepped down from the veranda. All at once, as if they shared a single brain, the birds raised their heads and turned to face her. Her heart raced. A rough hand gripped her shoulder and before she knew it, she was back inside the homestead.

"What were you doing?" Asked George, "You'll catch your death out there."

"I thought," said Mary, "Nothing. Sorry. Still half asleep."

There was concern in the farmhand's eyes. Mary refastened her gown and ran a hand through her wet morning hair, desperate to tame the mess. Peering out the window the field was empty once more, the birds and rats scattered to the wind. *They were just... Am I imagining things?*

"There's a leak coming down in the hay store," said George, "Don't think we'll be able to ride this one out in the barn."

"Of course," she stuttered, pulling herself away from the glass, "Best you both stay in here until it passes."

"Appreciate it."

Big Tom came stomping back through, his hands relieved of all but one of the beer bottles, he still wore his workman's boots and clumped mud prints stained her floors with each step he took. Flashes of the midnight markings filled her mind, these were similar, very similar, but undoubtedly different. *Who was it?*

"Mar'? You sure you're alright?"

George's voice broke her fixation, she raised her head and nodded, "I'm fine."

"Good," the farmhand placed his hand on her shoulder again, "We've taken care of everything we could, livestock are safe, and we've boarded up what we can."

His hand was strong and calloused, with faded cuts across the knuckles and thick raised veins. Her gaze lingered on it, and he quickly pulled it away.

"I'm sorry," said Mary, "Still in a bit of shock..."

There was a hiss from a beer bottle as Big Tom flung a cap loose, "No worries," said the giant, he swung his head back and drained most of the bottle in a single gulp, "It's what you pay us for."

Here's hoping I can still pay after this storm passes. We're already pushing our luck with such sickly crops.

A flash of yellow lit the homestead, the rumble of thunder followed close on its heels. Mary's grip on her gown tightened. The growl that chased the lightning sounded the same as the slope when it fell.

"Lilith!" Mary shouted, "Come here sweetheart."

She rushed to the stairs. There was another crackle, then for a blink the homestead shone as bright as day. When the thunder came, the whole house shook. Timber and stone shifted from the foundation. Mary fell against the banister and the tight flesh about her foot felt as though it had been torn anew.

"Lilith!" She cried.

George came up behind her and echoed the call, "Lilith?"

"Yes Mumma?"

Her little girl sauntered out to the head of the staircase, seemingly without notice or care of the chaos raging around them. Mary took Lilith in her arms.

She did not have the strength to bury another loved one, if there was to be another tragedy her family would all share the same fate. Lilith would remain close by, and they would survive or perish together.

Everyone convened in the parlour. Lilith and Big Tom sat by the window watching the destruction outside, while George read from the Bible, and Mary tried her best to appear calm. She could feel the homestead being pushed by the gale. The sound of nails separating from wood and hail slamming against the tin roof stung her ears. Leaks sprouted all over and Mary raced about placing pots and pans underneath to catch the rainfall. It did not take long until she ran out of cookware and was left with no choice but to watch as the floorboards soaked.

The morning passed slowly, with Mary doing her best to create chores for herself to keep her mind occupied. Remaining busy proved challenging, she could only stand for so long before the aching in her swollen foot became too much and forced her to rest. Lilith and Tom seemed to have little concern for the storm and passed the time shooting marbles together while the big man drank as though he were trying to blackout and sleep through the whole ordeal.

As lunch time rolled around and stomachs began to growl, Mary served up a cold lunch of leftover rabbit's pie, sliced bung fritz and cuts of buttered rye. Tom argued for a larger meal, but Mary refused him. *We could be stuck inside for days; I won't risk starving.*

Harsh winds belted the sides of the homestead and endless rain seeped in through gaps and cracks with each passing moment. The kitchen table had to be dragged halfway into the sitting room to avoid all the fresh leaks. Lilith sat at the head, Big Tom beside her and George down the far end. Once everyone had been served a plate Mary fixed one for herself and sat down in one of the middle chairs. As she took her seat thunder rumbled, and a fresh assault of hail smashed against the tin like a sledgehammer. She rested her elbows on the table and interlocked her fingers, "Let's ask for mercy from this storm. Who wishes to say grace?"

"Always happy to Mar," said George, mirroring her and folding his hands in prayer.

Jumping up on her seat, Lilith waved her hands back and forth, "Me Mumma, me!"

George nodded to her with a small smile. "Alright then," said Mary.

Lilith folded her hands and squeezed her eyes tight. Big Tom polished off his bottle with a burp then did the same.

"Bless us, O God." Lilith's words came slow, with drawn out pauses in the middle as though she was just barely able to remember them, "Bless our food and drink. Thy gifts from which we are about to receive from Thy bounty. And please keep us safe from the storm."

Mary opened her mouth to say amen but was cut off by the prayer continuing, "And bless Father Dirt, for warning us of the storm. Amen."

Big Tom joined the child in closing the prayer, Mary and George did not. Lilith and the giant went to work on their plates. Mary raised her cutlery for a moment then placed them back on the table, "I told you this Father Dirt business needs to stop," she said, "You're insulting your dad and the Lord with this make believe now."

"Father Dirt's real," said Lilith, "He talks to me all the time."

"You think that," said Mary, "I heard voices and had imaginary friends as a girl too, but it's all pretend."

"My nanna reckoned she saw a ghost one night," interrupted Big Tom with a mouthful of pie and fritz, "On 'er way out to the dunny, maybe this is something like that."

For that, the big man received a glare as sharp and piercing as a pitchfork. "Ghosts aren't real," said Mary, "And neither is Father Dirt."

"Knew about the storm though."

"A strange coincidence," said George, "But still a coincidence."

"I heard you talk to him Mumma," said Lilith, "By the stone while I play, you say all sorts of things."

"That's different," Mary sighed, "The departed can hear us up in Heaven, but they can't speak back."

"Father Dirt speaks back."

Mary pushed herself back from the table and stood up, the chair squealed as it scuffed along the floor, "Enough! Matthew can't talk to us, and I'll have no more of the topic."

A stab of pain shot up from Mary's mangled foot. No one spoke another word, but they all stared. Her anger dwindled quickly, replaced by embarrassment for losing her temper. The outburst was not all for naught though, as she stood over her household looking down at their uncomfortable faces Mary realized, *foolish to debate with a child, best way to end this Father Dirt nonsense is to stomp out any mention of it.*

Mary straightened her dress and hair then slowly eased back down into her seat, "There'll be no more outings to The Pile and if I hear that name again, I'll be washing your mouth clean with soap."

"That's not fair!" Cried Lilith.

"Nothing is," snapped Mary, "Now let's finish our lunch."

The men resumed eating, Lilith did not. The rest of the meal was a quiet affair, Mary did her best to force smiles and keep conversation going but having to be the angry mother had ruined her mood. George made up for much of her mental absence with a mixture of cheesy jokes and stories from back home. Big Tom mostly opened his mouth to either laugh, eat, or drink. He polished off five bottles during the meal alone. Less than an hour after eating, he was slumped over the couch fast asleep, drool running down his chin and a snore that competed with the storm winds bellowing out of him.

Lilith remained seated at the table, in the throws of a silent tantrum. In time, her angered expression fell, and she too drifted off into the peace of an afternoon nap.

Mary was left alone with George to pass the time; they spent the afternoon talking about life over cups of tea and games of checkers. She resisted any further discussions about her daughter's disobedience and George, being a gentleman, never pushed the course. There was plenty to discuss without it and conversation never seemed to lag.

The storm broke not long after the clock struck seven. The sun was just starting to slip beneath the horizon and surveying the farm in the waning light was too difficult. Instead, Mary led Geroge upstairs and the pair moved between bedrooms inspecting the farm from the windows. The rooms smelt of damp jumbuck and the floors were covered with dusty puddles.

Outside, fallen trees and hefty branches littered the pathways and lanes. Nearly a dozen fences had been either flattened or ripped out of the ground entirely. The crops were washed out, and a considerable portion of the barn's roof had caved in, leaving behind a carriage sized hole. The Pile remained as tall and solid as ever.

Mary pointed down towards the barn, "Looks like you'll be sleeping up here for a while."

"Won't be a cheap fix," said George, "We were already looking at a smaller harvest."

"I'll figure it out. Always have."

The sun soon fell behind the shattered tree line and moonlight proved too feeble to discern much of anything outside. Mary slunk back from the window and down onto the edge of her bed, "There's always something," she said, "No matter how hard we work, how good of a harvest we have, there's always something to take it away."

She looked out to The Pile, "I haven't managed enough for a new dress since Matthew passed," she said, "How many men do you think it would take to bring the dirt down?"

"I don't know," said George, "It'd depend on how fast you'd want the job done."

"Is this it?" Mary sighed, "Are we just meant to sit on this hill until it's our time too?"

George sat down beside her. "You've had some rough years," he said, "But you've only just started Mar', there's all the time in the world for new dresses and to see your husband taken care of. Even if you end up broke and destitute, you'll be alright, you've got a bright daughter, a loyal friend in Tom and... Me, I care about you Mar' and no matter what storms are ahead we'll help you through them."

Tears formed in the corners of her eyes as a smile rose, "Thank you," she said taking his hand in hers and squeezing, "You're a good man."

"You make it easy."

Suddenly Mary took notice of her surroundings, she was alone in her bedroom with a man other than her husband. She pulled her hand back and got to her feet, "We should check on the others," she said.

"Of course."

On their way out of the room George stopped at her bedside table and lifted up the copy of *The Turn of the Screw* that he had lent her, "How're you liking it?" He asked.

Mary looked into his kind face and couldn't find the words to tell him that with the mental burden and lack of sleep of the past few days she hadn't managed to get through more than a couple pages. "It's good," she said, "Excellent choice as always."

George inspected the book, almost as if he was back in the store and considering the purchase, "Ghosts are all well and good for the story books Mar," he said, "But we'd best be sure they stay there. Just because the dead can't speak doesn't mean they can't haunt us."

"Trust me," said Mary, "That I know all too well."

Chapter Four

The next morning, before the first rooster had cawed, Mary was up working in the kitchen by candlelight, kneading the dough for the days baking. The new day had seen the return of the summer heat, and an unpleasant humidity plagued the homestead. She dreaded how much worse it would get once the sun finally rose.

She could feel the exhaustion of the past few days in the tightness of her face. The moonlight made faint mirrors of the kitchen windows through which she could see the deep-set bags underneath her eyes, they were puffed and purple like fresh bruises. To her, she looked as bad as Big Tom when he'd get into squabbles over unpaid gambling debts down at the public house. *At least I don't have the swollen knuckles too,* she thought.

There came a rapping at the front door. As she approached, she could hear the chitter chatter of what sounded like a small mob outside. Easing the door open revealed Miss Mackenzie alongside the town priest Father Bowdern with a little over a dozen Yahl locals at their backs, each dressed in their Sunday best and holding candle lit lanterns that cast long moving shadows across their tired faces.

At the sight of her, the crowd erupted into a frenzy of questions, each of which only served to drown out the others. Through the shouting, words and phrases such as Father Dirt, miracle, and child saviour stood out, but little more than that could be decerned. The commotion caused her brow to grow heavy and her head to ache. She was about to snap, curse the lot of them, and slam the door, when a stretched out shush climbed up over the wall of noise and levelled it to an uneasy silence; it was Father Bowdern.

The seventy-year-old was dressed in his usual garb of an oil black suit. A pyrite cross hung from his neck, and he was clutching a blood red bible against his chest. Most of his ghost white hair was hidden beneath a wide brimmed hat, but the beginnings of his central bald spot remained visible. "Come now," the priest instructed, "We don't wish to frighten the poor woman."

Mary massaged her temples, "It takes more than this to frighten me," she told him.

The old man smiled, "Of course my dear."

"To what do I owe the pleasure father?"

"A miracle!" Miss Mackenzie's shrill voice spoke in place of the priests', "Your Lilith has been blessed."

"You interrupt my morning for this nonsense?"

"Our Matthew speaks again," the spinster insisted, "With God's grace and the love of his own child, he's come back to us a new as Father Dirt. He must have so much to tell us, so much to teach us."

Murmurs of approval came from the nearby flock as Mary tried her best not to pull a sour face. *Our Matthew, Father Dirt. That gibfaced windbag.* She'd never heard someone outside the farm say the words "Father Dirt" before; Lilith's fairytale was spreading. Mary had told herself she'd ignore any allusions to the name, *easy enough when dealing with a child, not so much with a geriatric.*

Mary fantasized about handling the old woman the way she had promised to deal with Lilith, wrapping her grey hair up in her fist and dragging her inside, forcing her over the sink and washing her mouth out with soap until she coughed on the bubbles. It was a harsh thought, quickly followed by guilt, but if she could've gotten away with it, she was almost certain she would have done it. *How dare she disrespect my husband.*

Father Bowdern's voice broke the silence, "This is what they say. Several of my flock have come to me, each telling the same story, they say your daughter spoke to her father from beyond the grave and he gave warning of the storm."

Mary sighed. She cast her eyes over the shrouded faces that darkened her doorstep, shocked that a little thunder and lightning was all it took to convince so many of a child's fable. "Thank you for the visit," said Mary, "But I am afraid you're all mistaken, there's been no miracle, just a naughty child playing games."

She moved to close the door, but was blocked by the outstretched arm of Father Bowdern, who wedged his bible into the door jam. "My child," he said, "I'm afraid I must insist you reconsider. This is not for you to decide, matters of the divine fall to the church."

He tried to push the good book deeper into the homestead, but Mary did not allow him to advance. The priest leaned in close and spoke in a whisper, "My dear, if this Father Dirt business is as you say and I am inclined to believe it is, we should disprove it now before speculation spreads and gives way to fanaticism. They want to see her speak to him, with all they lost yesterday and the hope the story gives, they are unlikely to relent. I propose we take little Lilith up to The Pile and let her commune. Give them what they want, and they will see just how ridiculous it all is."

Mary let the priest's words fall to silence as she considered them. Reluctantly she peeled the door back, "Fine. She won't listen to me, maybe you'll be able to show her reason."

"Splendid!" Miss Mackenzie called out from the edge of the veranda. *How'd the old bat hear us from back there?*

"Ten minutes," Mary insisted, "Not a second more. She's meant to be grounded."

The spinster smiled, exposing a web of hidden wrinkles along her face, "That's all the time we need dear," she said, "The Lord has performed greater miracles than Father Dirt with less."

With gritted teeth, Mary retreated inside. She knocked gently before entering her daughter's bedroom, it wasn't needed, Lilith was already up and dressed, standing by the window. Mary spoke to her child's back, "They're here for you," she said, "They want to take you up to The Pile. They expect a miracle."

Lilith said nothing. To ease the discomfort of the silence Mary began looking about the room, at the clothes and toys, at the drawings pinned against the walls. *Matthew would be proud.* "I still remember when I told your father we were expecting you," said Mary, "He didn't sleep for three days he was so excited. Me and Tom joked that the farm was going to go bankrupt from all the free drinks he was buying, he brought everyone in, the whole town celebrated like it was Christmas... That's who I want everyone to think of when they think of your father, not some ghost in the dirt. Not a topic of gossip. Not a joke. This story of yours, Father Dirt, it's slipping beyond our control. Words spread fast in small towns like ours and they change and twist just as quick, the town will turn on us if you keep lying to them. Today they're demanding you go up on the dirt, who knows what they'll be forcing upon us a week or a month from now. You need to listen to me Lilith. You need to stop this."

Lilith remained as quiet as the grave. "I've been harsh these past few days," Mary admitted, her bottom lip quivering and her eyes beginning to water, "I hate it as much as you, but I do it to protect you and your father. End this and let's get back to how things used to be. Do the right thing sweetheart."

Her little girl stayed silent and staring, looking out at the farm below. Mary could feel herself shaking as she waited for her to speak. Deep breaths did little to calm her. Finally, with a sympathetic tone to her voice, Lilith spoke, "I will Mumma."

Mary sighed with relief, "Good," she said, "Very good. Fetch your bonnet, we don't have time to do your hair."

Lilith retrieved a pale purple bonnet from the dresser, it did not match her dress, but Mary let it be. If she was going to stop with the games, Lilith could wear her nightgown for all she cared.

There was applause and cheers as mother and daughter stepped out onto the veranda. In all her years living in Yahl Mary had never seen the people so excited, so full of hope, nothing about their demeanour let on that most likely faced financial ruin in the wake of the storm. *When your only way out is a miracle, I suppose you either go mad or start believing in fairytales.* It brought her no joy to know she was about to crush what little hope they had left.

Miss Mackenzie pushed up past everybody and hunched down in front of Lilith, "This is exciting, isn't it?" she said, "You're special my dear."

Lilith smiled and gave a polite nod. Stepping between them, Mary ushered her daughter away, down to the veranda's edge where Father Bowdern was resting against a post. "Well father? Are we doing this?" Mary asked.

The priest eased up to his feet and waved his bible in the air as if it were a crier's bell, "Onward everyone," he shouted, "Let us see if God's blessing awaits us!"

The congregation moved down the slope. Puddles sloshed under foot and fallen twigs and branches snapped with a crackling sound like that of a wishbone from a Christmas chicken. Mary paid close attention to everyone's feet as they walked, particularly to the prints their boots left behind in the mud. None matched the intruders.

Halfway down the front yard clearing, the outhouse door swung open and Big Tom came stumbling out, still visibly tipsy from the night before. His shirt was half buttoned, and his suspenders hung down by his knees. Father Bowdern called out to him and like any priest worth his salt attempted to sway the drunken man to his side. "Will you join us my son?" The old man asked, "We seek the glory of God."

The priest's words made Mary uneasy. The father claimed this was all to disprove Lilith's story, surely an educated man of the faith did not expect to hear a dead man speak. *It must be for show,* she told herself, *He cannot appear too dismissive without proper evidence, else his followers may turn on him.*

It never took much to convince Tom to join in. He ran up and joined the procession as it neared the upper paddock. Out in the field they spotted George, dragging a branch off a flattened fence. Father Bowdern called to him, "I recognize you boy. Third pew on the right, every Sunday. Will you be coming to witness the Lord's work too?"

"Afraid not father, I'm busy cleaning up the Lord's work from yesterday."

Mary did her best to hide a chuckle. "He should mind his tongue," hissed Miss Mackenzie into the father's ear.

"In toil there is profit," he told her, "We can hardly fault the boy for working. He's more pious than most his age, I'm sure he meant no harm."

More pious than most anyone, Mary thought.

"I'll speak with him a moment, see if he won't come around."

The priest halted the mass and waddled further down to George. On the verge of earshot, Mary strained to hear their conversation.

"You should be careful son, speaking of the Lord in such a manner."

"I meant no offence... And I'll have an easier time seeking forgiveness than the rest of you."

"We need no forgiveness."

"If you go up to that dirt you will. I don't hold any papers of divinity like yourself father, but my minds sharp and I read well enough. Bible's clear, trying to speak with the dead is an abomination."

"You're right, you hold no papers of divinity. Many a man can read the good book, but few can understand it. Communion with outside forces is not the most honourable pursuit but look over my shoulder son. A dozen today, who knows how many a week from now. Men will believe whatever suits them best. A new century is upon us and with it a hunger for change. If we're not careful, if we shy away from everything we do not understand, our Lord's good word will be lost in the mire of progress and new age beliefs."

"There's nothing up there but bugs and dirt, only a fool would believe any different."

"You hold a low opinion of your fellow townsmen."

Father Bowdern placed a hand on the young man's shoulder, "I suspect you're right, but only a true fool makes his judgements without evidence."

"I've all the evidence I need."

"We shall see."

The priest aimed his bible towards The Pile and the group moved on, down to the paddock's edge where the fence had been ripped out of the ground and laid trampled in the mud. Mary hoisted Lilith onto her hip and carried her over. She moved cautiously, fearful that shattered glass still laid in wait. Even with her boots on the cut could still be felt and fear of reopening the wound filled her mind with dread.

The upper paddock was a torn-up mess and trudging through it was exhausting. Mud reached up everyone's shins and more than a few boots were sucked loose and lost to the muck. Father Bowdern and Miss Mackenzie both required assistance crossing. Big Tom helped ease the old woman's burden and a pair of young ladies, Grace and Lillie Hart, sisters from a nearby dairy farm, lent the priest their hands, though to Mary's eyes the father made more use of the girl's shoulders and hips than anything else. Before long everyone made it across to the outer paddock and The Pile.

The dirt was still damp and coated in a thin glossy sheen. It reeked, not of its usual earthy smell, but that of an open grave infested with mould and rot. Mary raised her blouse up over her nose and mouth, she was the only one. The townsfolk were entranced by the imposing mound. A day ago, it would not have received a second glance but now it prompted audible gasps from some in the crowd. *I could shovel pig shit under their noses and they'd still smile.*

It was hard not to feel offended, nary a soul had turned up to lay flowers or pay their respects since the unveiling of Matthew's memorial. But now that they felt there was something to be gained, they could not be kept away.

With the dirt in front of her, Mary started to reconsider letting Lilith go up. The smell was putrid, the rainwater only served to make the dirt seem even less clean. "Perhaps we should wait for another day," Mary suggested, "I don't think it's safe so soon after a storm."

"Nonsense," argued the spinster, "A little damp never hurt anyone."

"We're already here," added Father Bowdern, "Best we see to it now."

The procession fanned out along the base of The Pile. Mary limped forwards and reluctantly lowered Lilith from her hip. Kneeling beside her daughter, she took her head in her hands, and kissed her cheek, "I love you," she said, "So does dad, even if he's not here to say it."

"I know Mumma," said Lilith, returning the kiss onto Mary's wrist.

Mary returned to the group. She wanted to leave but did not trust the crowd of fanatics around her to be left alone with her daughter. When Mary had summited The Pile with no hesitation and a sliced foot the night before the storm, she gained some false confidence and for a moment believed her anxieties had left her, only now did she realize that was not the case. *Don't make a scene,* she told herself as her nerve started to fault. She crossed her arms and hugged herself tight to keep from shaking. Her fingers danced around the small of her back, the same way Matthew's used to when he would hold her. *Relax wombat, everything works out in the end.*

As Lilith stepped to the dirt Father Bowdern called for her to stop. The priest waddled up to her side, hunched himself over and whispered some unheard words into her ear. Lilith nodded and went right to climbing as Father Bowdern moved to rejoin the line. Confused, Mary called to him, "What did you say to her?"

"Just wishing her luck my dear," insisted the priest.

Goodluck is a private conversation?

As she watched her little girl climb, Mary noticed a spattering of black and white feathers sticking out of The Pile. She'd nearly forgotten about the rats and magpies, the animals strange behaviour seemed so trivial with all the stresses and hardships left in the storm's wake. Still, it was odd, and Mary could not fully shake the uneasiness she'd felt at the sight of them. *We all go a bit mad in a storm,* she told herself, *even birds and rats aren't immune.*

Lilith reached the summit. There was no grand spectacle like the gathered had hoped, her little girl simply started to play as any other child would. Dancing about and humming songs to herself as she kicked up clumps of dirt. After a few minutes of nothing happening, the crowd started to murmur, *they're realising their mistake.*

As if prompted by their scepticism Lilith plunged both her hands down into the peak, raised up two fistfuls of moist dirt and started rubbing the muck all over her face, smooshing it into her delicate ears.

"Lilith," Mary cried out, "Stop that, you'll get an infection."

Several in the crowd shooshed her. "Don't quieten me," Mary yelled, "She's my daughter!"

"She's fine," called out an unknown man.

"Let her work dear," added Miss Mackenzie.

Mary shook her head and limped forward, ready to climb. A tug on her wrist brought her back, it was Big Tom. "Give 'er a minute," he said, "If she does anything too silly, I'll fetch her ma self."

The big man loosened his grip and took Mary's hand in his, above them Lilith continued spreading the grime about her face and ears. The child made no sound, other than the faint humming of a familiar but unplaceable tune.

With gritted teeth, Mary waited the full ten minutes she had promised. Lilith did not speak a single word, only made a mess of herself. As she was about to call her down, there was a burst of noise from the summit, "I hear you!" the little girl shouted.

A chilled gust of wind, a remanent of the passing storm, swept across the outer paddock and sent a chill to Mary's bones. The distant squawking of plover birds and the chirping of unseen insects vanished. No one said a word. No one made a sound. Everyone looked to Lilith.

The child pressed both hands against her ears and flung herself back and forth, groaning and shrieking, wailing at the top of her lungs. Mary looked to Big Tom, "Help her."

The big man jumped into the dirt, just as the noises stopped and Lilith's body became straight and rigid. Whispers permeated the crowd. Men stripped their hats from their heads and held them to their chests. Miss Mackenzie smiled wide. Father Bowdern glanced about the crowd.

"Father Dirt says!" Lilith shouted.

Mary's heart skipped a beat. *No, she promised.*

"Father Dirt says no one listened to him," Lilith continued, "But he's not mad cause now everyone knows he's telling the truth. He says the righteous don't need to be told twice."

Applause broke out across the paddock and Tom slunk back from off The Pile.

"He says everyone should call him Father Dirt from now on—"

"Stop this," Mary shouted, "Stop this right now!"

Those beside her hissed at her to be quiet. Mary rushed forwards towards the mound, but several spectators blocked her. "Tom," she cried out.

Big Tom gave them a stern look. Their faces dropped, and fear filled their eyes. "Lay a hand on her," he said, "And I'll break 'em."

Mary was allowed to pass, but before she could reach the dirt, Tom grabbed her hand once more, "You won't get up there quick enough to stop 'er," he said, "Let the little lady say her piece, might do 'er some good."

Lilith's sermon continued, "You didn't listen, but you can still be saved, Father Dirt knows the way. He knows the secrets of the land. He knows where to find gold—"

Gasps jolted out from the crowd as they looked amongst themselves in excitement, their eyes already counting the hypothetical riches. "No more," Mary said to Tom, "These fools are buying this nonsense."

"Off Caroline Road," Lilith continued, "In the abandoned fields by the fallen pine trees, that's where to dig. Father Dirt says he gives you this gift so you can rebuild what was lost in the storm. Father Dirt loves us all, listen and all will be well."

Mary wrenched her hand free from Tom's, but Lilith had already finished. The little girl removed the clumps of dirt from her ears, crumbled them in her fingers and tossed the powder out onto the enthralled spectators below. Dirt sprinkled down like drifting ash from a bushfire. Two women rushed forwards to catch the falling grains like it was sacrament, giggling to one another like schoolgirls, they used the gathered filth to dust their foreheads. Cheers and hugs went all around.

From out of the celebration, Father Bowdern strode forward and plunged a foot into the soil, raising his hands to the sky, he called out in a booming voice as though he were in the midst of Sunday mass. "Brothers and sisters!"

There was quiet.

"I came here today as a sceptic, eager and ready to disprove this miracle. For that, I hope the good Lord can forgive me. When our angel Lilith spoke, I could feel something greater than ourselves— I have felt the Lord here with us today and I have felt Matthew, I have felt the presence of Father Dirt!"

The crowd cheered. The priest held a moment, then continued, "All of our devotion has brought us divine blessings. A father taken too soon, returned to us through his daughter, returned to give riches to the faithful man. If we strike gold where he has claimed and I am certain we shall, then there can be no doubt that Father Dirt is indeed a miracle sent to us from the heavens!"

Whistles and chants of "Father Dirt" broke out. Lilith basked in the adoration and Father Bowdern feasted on her scraps. Mary stood frozen, gazing up at her daughter through a shower of dirt. *How could I have let this happen?*

Chapter Five

Over a fortnight had passed since Lilith last stepped foot on The Pile, despite the best efforts of the little girl and the town. Day and night huddled masses of believers darkened her doorstep, praying and pleading for the mother to let her daughter come outside. They tried everything to sway her, free labour, purses full of coin, one man had even offered a prized pig. Mary refused them all. *Betray my husband for a swine, they must think I'm an idiot.*

She knew for a fact that, following the storm, some of these trespassers did not even have a roof over their heads. Yet here they were, willing to part with the last of their money just to see a child play in the dirt. Their own children would starve come winter.

The scorching summer sun lingered on the horizon, a bloody smear that had long outstayed its welcome. The air inside the homestead was thick and suffocating. Sweat soaked Mary's stockings and the pits of her blouse. She contemplated kicking off her shoes to at least give her feet some relief, but thought better of it, she hated being reminded of her newly acquired scar. George had formed a habit of telling her not to fret and to instead be grateful that it wasn't tetanus; he was right as he often was, but it was still a struggle not to mourn the perceived loss of beauty she had suffered.

Mary sat at the kitchen table alongside Lilith and George. She'd prepared a cold supper of silverside, chopped fruits, vegetables, and buttered rye. Three place settings, the same tonight as every night since Lilith's declaration of gold.

Like most of Yahl's able-bodied men, Big Tom had spent just about every free second down Caroline Road digging. He had been swept up in the fervour, an overnight believer. The big man had a big heart, but a small brain, and Mary had little doubt that they'd only needed to promise him a supply of booze and tobacco to sway him to their side. *A man of vices is a man easily bought.*

Mary and George shared their days with one and other as they ate, while Lilith sat in silence. She'd been strictly watched, confined to the homestead following the incident and the child wasn't taking it well. Mary had tried to lift her girl's spirits, but it was an impossible task without bowing to her principles. Lilith had caused a lot of grief for Faulds Farm and Mary worried about the troubles to come when the town realized there was no gold to be found.

A fortnight's worth of labour wasted, she thought, *with all that time and effort spent chasing a little girls fancy they probably could've seen to most of the storm's destruction already. Or they could've used their picks and shovels to take down The Pile, give Matthew the proper burial he deserves.*

There'd been a chance for that. Mary had suggested the idea to one of the more devout groups who approached her, but Lilith had suffocated that plan in the crib. From her bedroom window the little girl shouted down, "Father Dirt doesn't want his pile disturbed. Father Dirt belongs to the ground; he belongs to Faulds Farm."

That was the most Mary had heard her speak all fortnight. The Pile remained untouched, but some wandered up to the outer paddock and attempted to clear away the thicker patches of weeds and brush. A kind gesture, but not enough to sway Mary from her beliefs.

Tonight, Lilith was as quiet as ever. All Mary's attempts to include the child in conversation ended the same way, a bitter blank stare.

George plucked a plum from his plate and held it up, "When I was a wean," he said, "Growing up on my Pa's farm, he had a whole orchard of plum trees."

"And believe it or not, some of his trees grew magic plums," he said, winking at Mary, "Pa taught me all the tricks, and you know what... These look awfully similar to Pa's magic plums."

George placed the plum into an open palm, "Look close."

Lilith leaned forwards as George formed a fist around the fruit. He raised his hand high over the table, blew into it, then unfolded his hand to reveal the plum had vanished. Lilith nearly jumped across the table. Mary clapped and quietly cheered.

George took a small bow, "That's some pumpkins, right? Shall I show you how to do it?"

Lilith nodded eagerly. George pulled out the chair beside him, "Come on then."

Her girl rushed to his side and Mary mouthed him a silent thank you. Lilith watched closely as the farmhand explained the intricacies of the trick to her. Mary found herself smiling as she watched, it felt like forever since she had smiled genuinely and not for social etiquette. The explanation lasted barely a minute, but she could have watched for hours. In those fleeting moments the problems of Father Dirt faded away and everything felt like it was going to be alright.

After listening to George's instructions, Lilith attempted the trick. "Look Mumma."

Her little girl stood up on her chair and with all the theatrics of a seasoned vaudeville star showed her empty hand. She placed a plum in the centre, same as George and with a giggling grin on her face balled her hand to a fist.

Squoosh! Lilith's expression turned to confusion as the sound of the plum turning to puree squeaked out from her hand and purple ooze seeped through her fingers.

Mary covered her mouth, trying to stifle a laugh. George turned into his shoulder to contain his amusement. Slowly, the little girl opened her hand to reveal a massacred piece of fruit, "What the..." She mumbled.

Both Mary and George broke in an instant, letting out a roar of laughter. Lilith soon joined in, and all three shared in the glee. Once they'd calmed down Mary wiped her daughter's hand with a tea towel and George gave her an encouraging pat on the back, "Alright," he said, "I think I know what went—"

A sudden merry shouting coming up the veranda cut George off. Before there could be any wonder as to who it was the front door came flying open and Big Tom bounded inside. He was smiling wide, flashing his mouthful of stained horse teeth. In his hands were three empty beer bottles, he stomped to the kitchen and tossed them into the bin with a clanging that sent a jolt up Mary's spine as she anticipated a shatter. "We did it," The giant proclaimed, "We struck gold!"

Mary jolted up half out of her seat, her eyes wide with shock and fixed on the big man, "No," she said, "You can't have."

Lilith leapt from her chair, knocking it to the floor as she went, "Told you! Told you! Told you!" She cheered as she danced around the table.

Big Tom mimicked the child's movements as he made his way further into the kitchen. "We 'ave," he called out.

"How much was found?" Asked George.

"Not a real lot." The sound of the big man rummaging through the cupboards and icebox could be heard as he spoke, "But we'll keep looking."

Tom came marching back into sight, back towards the door, holding several opened beer bottles in one hand and paper wrapped packages of sliced meats and cheese in the other. "There'll be plenty more," he said, "Father Bowdern reckons finding a little means there's a lot about."

"We can hope," said George.

There was a hint of confusion in the young man's voice, Mary felt it too. *Pet names, weather changes, that's nothing really, but gold, how does a child know of gold? Is it possible she really can speak with him?* Mary quickly shook the thought from her head. *You can't speak with the dead. It could have been planted, or this is all just some extraordinary luck. There will be a rational explanation.*

A tug on her sleeve drew Mary's attention, Lilith had ceased her dancing and now stood at her side with the same wide grin on her face as Tom, "Father Dirt was right," she said, "I told you."

"Good thing we listened," said Tom as he started for the front door.

"Where—" Mary stuttered, "Where are you going? Why are you taking our food?"

"The party! Bunch a people outside. They wanted to celebrate the gold and Father Dirt, so I tell 'em they should come over."

Mary tensed up. She owed Tom a lifetime of gratitude and exemptions for all the work he'd done following Matthew's passing to keep Faulds Farm alive, and he seemed intent on collecting all of the debt. She'd spent weeks sobbing in bed, he'd seen the season through on his own and broken more than one banker's nose when the threats of repossession started. Despite all he'd done, whenever he came home from a night's drinking soaked in piss and sick, that Mary knew she would have to clean, or offered up hospitality that was not his to offer, she could not help but feel the urge to strike him upside the head with the skillet. She resisted the urge, as she always had and always would.

"I wish you would've talked to me first," she said, straining her face to a smile she hoped appeared natural, "I could've prepared something more substantial. Made exceptions in the budget for guests."

"No one cares 'bout all that, we're 'bout a be rich!"

Tom raised his arms and shook them like a triumphant sportsman, beer spittle and meat juices dripped down him as he celebrated and puddled up along the freshly swept floor. "Youse all have to come out to The Pile," The big man continued, "This is like history bein' made."

"Can we Mumma?" Lilith asked, "We have to."

It was difficult to say no to an excited child, but Mary had managed to do so for the past two weeks, and she had no intention of breaking now. The notion of Father Dirt had to be killed and Matthew returned. There was no better way to ruin any chance of that than to take her little girl up to The Pile during a party to celebrate the imagined saint. "I don't think so," said Mary, "You've shown you can't be trusted up there."

"Pretty please?" The child crossed her hands in prayer and fluttered her big doe eyes like a barn cat begging for a saucer of milk.

"C'mon Mary," chided Tom, "This is probably the best thing that'll ever 'appen to this place, you should enjoy it. Everyone's out there, she'll be good."

Mary's eyes sank to the three half eaten plates on the table. *What a lovely meal we were having.* "No," Mary insisted, "I'm sorry but there'll be no more of this nonsense, Lilith and I will be staying right here."

Lilith scrunched up her face until tears formed in the corners of her eyes. The big man shook his head. "Mary," he said. "You might not like the way they're doing it, but the whole town is out there to celebrate your fella. They're all here to pay respects to a good and decent man, my best friend. I'd probably be dead by now without him... You want to forget what happened and that's up to you, you're his wife, you can do as ya like, but I want a chance to have one last drink with my mate and his family. Can I have that?"

Mary had never seen the big man be so serious or speak so eloquently. *Perhaps I owe him this much.* There was a long silence before she finally spoke, "Alright," she sighed, "We'll go."

Lilith and Tom both jumped for joy at her capitulation. *Please be a good visit. Don't breakdown in front of the whole town.*

"But," she continued, "There will be rules. First, you will listen and follow whatever I say and second, you will not set foot on that dirt. Do you understand?"

"I understand Mumma."

Lilith rushed outside; Big Tom followed close behind. Mary turned to George, "Fancy a party?"

The young man smiled, "I could be convinced."

Side by side they followed the others outside. The sun had finally taken its leave and darkness crept up Fauld's Farm. From the veranda she could see a river of candlelight streaming through the front gate and snaking its way up the front yard slope. The mass moved with good cheer; backed by the sounds of unfettered laughter and an off-tune violin. Amidst the sea of glowing beads, hunched shadows carried chairs and tables, crates of food and drink and garden game necessities. Near the top of the hill, the procession veered off through the fields towards the outer paddock. Mary tried to count the lanterns, but there were too many, she guessed that at least two hundred head must have passed through her gates.

She took in the sight, but Lilith and Tom had no such interest and without waiting for her or George they made a mad dash to join in the fun. *All this for a little girl's game.*

George stepped down to the dirt and offered Mary his hand, "Shall we?"

She needed no such help over such a small drop but happily took it anyway. "Thank you for in there," she said as the pair walked, "It was great— Good thing your Pa taught you about those magic plums."

"Happy to help," George chuckled, "It comes in handy. I wish you could've met him; you'd have loved him."

"If he was anything like his son, I know I would."

The outer paddock was a frenzy of noise and activity as they approached. Shouted conversations, children screaming, and raucous fiddle music filled the air. Men rushed about setting up tables and chairs, and dragging felled branches to a heap at the fields centre. Women set the tables full of food and drink. Elders, along with some of the younger women placed bouquets of garden roses around Matthew's memorial plague. *Tom might be right, maybe this won't be so bad after all.*

The gathered branches were arranged into a crude teepee shape that stood nearly two men high and set ablaze. A burst of orange engulfed the wood as flames took shape. Puffs of embers erupted into the clear night's sky before drifting back down and fading into the darkness. The heat was an unwelcome addition to an already blistering evening, but the bonfire provided a dull glow that lit the festivities.

A ring of mismatched chairs from various dining sets and porch steps around Yahl formed around the fire, along with a couple of hay bales and overturned buckets. Behind the circle was a spattering of tables, one for food and several for the evening's libations, alcohol made up most of the spread, but both old man Byrne and the widow Clarke cast tin cans over the edge of the blaze and prepared pots of Billy tea for those less inclined to drink the heavy stuff.

Games sprouted up around the field like weeds. A casual match of battledore and shuttlecock enraptured a group of older women, a group of teenage boys placed a large chunk of stone atop a distant fence post and started up a game of Duck on the Rock, and a couple small games of beanbags played out closer to the fire. Most attention however went to the tug of war match that was forming. A long rope was laid out a dozen yards down from the food and beverages, Big Tom stood at one end and Mary watched in amusement as the teams formed and all the waiting men tried to casually step to Tom's side of the rope.

Lilith had joined in with some of the local children, they ran about in a pack shouting, playing some game Mary had never heard of before, the sight delighted her. She hoped playing with other kids might dull the excitement around Father Dirt. The young ones were being followed around the paddock by Miss Mackenzie and the most devout of the dirt followers, they drank cups of mulled wine and spoke loudly of gold and gospel.

A patch of flattened crabgrass had been turned into a dance floor. A lone fiddle player cycled through the standards as couples danced the two step and the kangaroo hop with youthful enthusiasm. After some time observing, George managed to convince her to join in on the waltz.

Mary interlocked her fingers with the rough calloused hand of the young farmer as the squeaking strings rose to a tune. George's hand came round and cupped her back as the pair started to step and spin to the rhythm. They did not move perfectly, and glancing around at the other dancers it appeared that they were the weak link in the chain, but as they continued to twirl about the field Mary stopped looking at the others and focused solely on George. She could feel the fire on her cheeks as a smile grew and they settled into a rhythm all of their own. Forwards. Backwards. Side to side. Their feet fell unevenly, but they fell together.

The couple's confidence grew with each cycle of the dance, they moved faster and with more passion. She felt as though she was floating, gliding about just above the grass. Faster and with more passion. George spun her around, the skirt of her dress flared out as she twirled, and the evening breeze washed over her. When she came back round and George caught her, her eyes slipped from him and caught sight of the dirt looming behind them.

Her smile evaporated in an instant. Momentum carried her through a few more steps before she came to a stop.

"Are you alright?" George asked.

She was frozen, stuck in place like a bug in tree sap. She looked straight through George and to The Pile. *I'm dancing on my husband's grave.*

"Mar'?" George jostled her shoulder.

"Sorry," she said, "I... I just need to sit down for a minute."

George offered his forearm to escort, but Mary waved him off, "I'm fine, you go have fun. We'll join back up later."

"If you're sure," said George, "I'll come check on you in a bit alright?"

Mary managed a nod as she wandered off through the tapestry of spiralling skirts and sweat soaked bodies that gyrated all around her. She bumped into a good many dancers but lacked the wherewithal for the appropriate apologies; finding a place to sit and calm herself was all that occupied her mind. Relief came down by the bonfire. The heat was proving too much for many and there were plenty of gaps in the ring of chairs. She took a seat in the most secluded section she could find.

Looking up through the curtain of flames at the dirt that dominated the field, sadness gave way to guilt. For a moment Matthew had vanished from her thoughts. She had forgotten him, and, in her lapse, she had joined in a celebration that mocked his memory.

Just when she felt as though she could not feel any worse, she spotted Father Bowdern shuffling towards her. With a drawn out groan the weary priest settled into an empty kitchen chair beside her. "Are you alright my dear?" He asked, placing a gnarled hand on Mary's thigh, "A pretty young thing such as yourself should not waste a party sitting with us old timers."

Mary kept her eyes on the old man's presumptuous hand, "Mother always told me that a priest never lies... That woman was wrong about everything, I don't know why I believed her on this."

"My child," the old man sighed, "I've been with the church for over fifty years, you can believe me when I say I would never do anything to disrespect the memory of a good Christian such as your husband."

"It's not a matter of believing you." With a hard tug Mary straightened her skirt and the old man's hand recoiled like a child touching the stove, "You did it, it's done!"

"I felt a presence... A presence I have not felt since the day I discovered my calling and joined the church."

"Describe this presence."

The priest appeared at a loss for words. Mary scoffed, "What's it matter, they all believe you. Your words as good as the gold they just dug up."

"This is a good thing, my dear—"

"Yes, good for you," Mary interrupted, "Your attendance will go through the roof. You're revered by everyone in town, most famous priest on the continent once word spreads. Australia's first saint. All thanks to a five-year-old."

"I am simply glad the Lord allowed your husband the chance to offer such a blessing, I need none of the credit."

"But you'll get it all the same."

The old man shook his head, and his jowls rippled, "Grief has blinded you my child. Do you not see what this all means? Not only is Matthew with us, but now we have proof, irrefutable proof of God, of heaven, of all of it. Now everyone can stop with useless follies, with meaningless distractions, with sin."

The priest cast an arm out and gestured to the party around them, "Once all these people understand what this means they can devote themselves fully to the church as God intended and lead pure lives under the Lord's guidance."

Your guidance, Mary might have said. She turned back to face the flames and the dirt that loomed large over it, "Even if Father Dirt was real, all it would prove is that you got to him first. There was never any talk of God or religion until you showed up."

"Just because it was not put to words does not mean it was not there."

"And just because a priest believes it, does not make it so."

A moment passed in silence.

"If?" Father Bowdern asked, "If Father Dirt is real? Even now, you doubt our miracle?"

"It's getting harder," Mary admitted, "Something has been off, I've seen signs, had disturbing dreams, nothing has felt normal these past weeks. But still, I cannot help but think that all of us are just ascribing weight and meaning to meaningless things. The storm, the boot prints, would any of us think much of it if it wasn't for this whole narrative of Father Dirt."

"And the gold? A girl of five unearthing riches without lifting a trowel would surely be noticed, regardless of Father Dirt."

"I don't have an answer for that, not yet. I cannot explain everything that's happened, but if you're telling me that it's all my husband's doing, that he's suddenly speaking from beyond the grave after all these years. That he's the first and only man to ever do so. I cannot accept that, how could I?"

The wood of Father Bowdern's chair creaked as he braced his knees and pulled himself up to his feet, "It is not our place to understand the Lord's work," he said sternly, "Only to know it when we see it. You should be careful my dear, you and that boy you have working for you, our Lord is forgiving but he will not accept blasphemy. Remember Deuteronomy, plague and sickness will cling to those who do not obey. Obey and accept Father Dirt, both of you."

The old man placed another unwelcome hand upon her, this time, her shoulder. "Perhaps you're unable to accept the blessing because you cannot accept that he has chosen to speak to his daughter, and not his wife."

Heat rose inside her, *he thinks he can insult me, threaten me?* Flashes of a fantasy filled her mind, of pushing the priest into the flames and watching him flail as his skin blackened and burnt away, as his bones turned to cinders. The thought vanished as quick as it came. She knew she could never do such a thing but felt terrible all the same. *He's still a man of God, it's a sin to wish him harm.*

The father shuffled away, disappearing in amongst a migrating herd of dirt followers; Mackenzie's chosen. The spinster led the pack of just over a dozen. Her posture hunched, and her pace slow. Mary thought little of it at first considering the woman's age, but then came a glimpse of familiar fabric sashaying by her side, Lilith's dress. The spinster was towing her little girl behind her, through the maze of chairs, towards The Pile. "Come along everyone," she shrieked, "Come along, our little angel is going to give us the word of Father Dirt."

Mary cut a path through the crowd to her daughter, "No!" She shouted as she grabbed Lilith's wrist, "We agreed, no dirt."

"Miss Mackenzie said it was okay," Lilith protested.

Mary glared into the old woman's eyes as she spoke, "She is not your mother. We're leaving."

She started to drag the girl away, but managed only a couple of yards before resistance from beyond her grip stopped her and spun her around. It was the spinster, latched onto Lilith like a leech. "Come on dear," said the old bag, "Where's the harm? Look at all the good she's done for us."

"Let go of my daughter," Mary's words came slow and as sharp as a razor, Mackenzie's face dropped, but her grip only tightened.

Everyone started turning toward the spectacle and the empty space around them shrunk. The spinster's posse gathered behind their matriarch with murmured questions about what was happening and what was to be done. The wrinkles about the old bag's eyes deepened as her sagged cheeks rose and her cracked, wine-stained lips twisted to a self-satisfied smile.

Bitch! How dare she lay a hand on my child. Lilith was Mary's blood, she'd given birth to and raised the girl on her own, no one had offered more than hollow words of sympathy before they realized she could be exploited. Mary's mind flashed to Matthew's pistol by her bedside. *Anyone who gets between a mother and her child is asking for death.* She could not imagine herself capable of murder, yet she enjoyed the thought all the same. Pressing the barrel against the hag's head. Watching the pious facade fade. Pulling the trigger.

"Relax dear," The spinster's voice pulled her back to reality, "It's only for a few minutes, let the girl speak."

A chorus of encouragement broke out amongst the town and Mary now realized just how surrounded she was. A wall of bodies so thick she could no longer see the bonfire, just faint pillars of rising smoke in the distance. Like trained parrots Mackenzie's lackies began chanting for Lilith and Father Dirt.

She was surrounded by an army of drunks. Through the chaos she saw George trying to push his way through, but he was quickly swallowed up by the crowd. Big Tom was nowhere to be found.

Hundreds were shouting, most of whom were grizzled men. Violence was in the air, and no one was there to protect her. Mary's grip on Lilith loosened. "Go on," she sighed.

Cheers and whistles went up all around. The spinster surrendered her grip on the child and started to clap. Mary wondered to herself if she could get away with clocking the old bag so long as she let Lilith climb, but before she had the chance to decide Mackenzie disappeared into a swarm of her followers.

"It's okay Mumma," said Lilith, "Father Dirt won't take long."

Lilith walked to the edge of The Pile, everyone followed. Bodies surrounded her little girl and Mary was pushed out of her reach. Through the huddled masses she saw Father Bowdern emerge by

Lilith's side, he whispered in her ear a moment, then vanished as quick as he appeared. *Again?*

Lilith sunk her shoes into the dirt and started her ascent as the mob spread out. The crowd's faces were rosy with drink and sunburn, they stretched across the shadow pile like a raw rash, heads tilted upward in silent observation, save for the occasional encouraging shout or sloshed sip of alcohol.

When Lilith reached the top, there was an outburst of applause and whistles. Her child basked in the adoration for a moment, then with overflowing palms of dirt, raised both hands above her head like Moses delivering the commandments. The field was overcome with silence.

Lilith rubbed her hands over herself, smearing fresh dirt in overtop the dried-out stains from the weeks prior. The trail of grime ran up the length of her, ending at her ears which were padded full of clumped soil.

Unlike the last time, there was no wait before the child spoke. "Everyone!" She cried out, "Listen to me!"

The crowd pressed themselves up onto their tippytoes, as though a few more inches of height would allow them to hear anything they wouldn't have already.

"Father Dirt is here," Lilith continued.

Beside Mary a teenage girl with a malmsey nose called out to The Pile, "I love you Father Dirt!"

"What does he say?" Shouted an unseen man.

"Father Dirt says..."

Her child raised an empty hand as though she was holding a beer mug. "Father Dirt says cheers!"

A wave of bottles went up all around, and with them the suffocating stench of unwashed underarm. Bellows of support rang out as drinks clinked with one another, and liquor spilled, drenching Mary in a mixture of cheap ale and backwood whiskey.

Lilith put a finger to her lips, and everyone stopped. If Mary had not seen it, she would have scarcely believed it, hundreds halted by the flick of a little girl's wrist. A chill shot up her spine and gooseflesh prickled up along both her arms. She had yet to taste alcohol this evening, but she found herself feeling tipsy and as though she might be sick. *How can I control a child who has a whole town at her beck and call?*

There was little chance to dwell on her new fear, as Lilith continued to speak, "Father Dirt says thank you for your support and faith. He is sorry... Sorry that he could not convince you of the storm, but he hopes that with the gold you will be able to survive to next harvest."

Looking around the crowd Mary spied George in the distance, a sour look blemished his usually chipper face, and he gripped hold of a cross necklace around his neck like his life depended on it.

"Survive and get a couple a kegs of piss," a slurred shout hollered from the crowd. Most laughed, but none as loud as Big Tom.

"But Father Dirt says that he doesn't just want Yahl to survive," Lilith continued, "He wants Yahl to thrive. He has given gold, but he has more to give. He says he knows where to find lots of riches, so much that everyone in Yahl will never have to work again!"

The crowd was deafening. Mary plugged her ears and hunched over to shield herself from the spilt drinks and thrown bottles. Some jumped up and down and danced around, others broke down in tears, but all were happy. All praised Father Dirt. Lilith did not silence them this time, she waited for them to simmer on their own, then continued. "All he asks," shouted Lilith, "All he asks before he blesses us, is for us to grant him one small favour."

"Anything!" cried Miss Mackenzie.

"He wants us to dig him a hole, right here, beside The Pile. He wants everyone to dig until he says stop. He wants me to visit every day and he will tell me when the work is done. When the hole is done, there will be a celebration to everyone's new lives, and he will tell us how to find the riches."

The crowd roared. There was no silencing them now and Lilith had to scream to be heard, "Dig for Father Dirt and be as rich as kings!"

"Father Dirt! Father Dirt! Father Dirt!"

Mary could not believe what she was seeing. She pinched at her wrist, but this was no dream. Lilith threw handfuls of dirt out over her followers. The most devout, the likes who clung to Mackenzie, rushed to the dust shower like debutants fighting for a flung bouquet. Some caught the dirt and pocketed it, some rubbed it over their faces like make-up, and others simply allowed it to wash over them.

Beyond the celebrating masses Mary caught sight of George storming off towards the homestead. She called to him, but there was no chance of him hearing her, she could barely hear herself. She turned back to The Pile.

"Lilith!" She screamed, "Lilith!"

Her shouts were not enough to break through the wall of noise, but they proved enough to quiet those close to her. When her voice rose again, it broke through, "Down!" she insisted, "Right now!"

To her surprise the girl listened. Showing no expression and with no resistance to Mary's demands, Lilith slid down The Pile. Mary pushed up to the dirt's edge and as soon as the girl was within reach grabbed her, placed her on her hip and began shoving her way out of the pack of people.

Questions and praise came from all directions, but the girl had no more words to speak. Many tried to grab her, but most got Mary instead. Dirtied fingernails clawed at her neck and groped her dress, she looked for the culprit's faces but couldn't distinguish any amongst the writhing mass. She struck many a hand with heavy slaps, but each time she knocked one away, two seemed to return to take its place.

Further down the paddock Mackenzie and her cronies tried to block the way, but Mary had none of it. She tucked her chin, lowered her shoulder, and charged through them. The old bag got out of the way in time, but they weren't all so lucky, Mary knocked an old jollocks to the weeds and dug her heel into a woman's shin as she broke through the line. Both cried as they fell, but Mary didn't care, she had a clear path to the homestead now and that was all that mattered.

She called back for Big Tom, "Dead the fire! Dead the fire and send everyone on their way now!"

The big man yelled back; she could barely make out a word but could tell by the cadence and tone that her message was received. As she fled across the paddock, the mob followed, "Get away!" Mary screamed, "Leave us be."

The flock surged towards them, shouting slurred prayers and demands as they pursued. Mary knew she could not outrun them with Lilith in her arms. Her mind raced trying to think of a way to escape. *I could threaten them with trespassing, or use Big Tom to muscle them out, maybe Lilith could calm them;* all ideas came in the matter of a couple of paces, but none were satisfactory.

Out of ideas and breath she felt herself slow, and the townsfolk gain on her. Suddenly it struck her. She turned to face the crowd with a raised hand, "Stop!" She shouted, "Father Dirt's family need their rest, anyone who does not leave will be mentioned to him by name tomorrow morning."

The crowd halted. Murmured voices gurgled up from unseen faces, but no words were made clear. A few stepped forward but made hasty retreats after only a couple steps. A moment passed then the mob turned back towards the dwindling bonfire. Apologies came from some, but most were silent or spoke only amongst those close to them. Speaking the false name made Mary feel ill, but she was free of the pursuit.

She burst into the homestead and dropped Lilith from her hip, "You promised me you'd listen!"

Creaking kitchen floorboards drew Mary's attention away from her daughter before the girl had a chance to answer. George was pacing back and forth, beer bottle in hand. The farmhand rarely drank and the sight of it filled Mary with unexplainable dread. She'd never been one for signs or superstitions, but this felt like an omen for worse to come.

She ordered Lilith to her room and the little girl skulked away with little complaint. "George," she said, inching towards the kitchen, "Are you—"

"This is not okay Mar'!" He yelled, "Not at all."

"What?" Mary asked.

He took a deep swig from his bottle, "Father Dirt."

The young man trembled as he spoke, as if he were suppressing a great rage, "I've held my tongue. She's your daughter, this is your land, but I'm not going to Hell for being too polite to say what needs to be said."

"George," she said, "I know this has all gotten out of hand, but—"

"No," George interrupted, "You don't, no one in this damned town seems to see how ludicrous this all is. I don't understand how the father hasn't seen this..."

"Bowdern is acting strange," continued Mary, "I think he's—"

"He's been blinded," George insisted, "Blinded by dreams of wealth and power. Turned a chancer. That's not what the church is about."

"No, but—"

"It's coming from under the ground Mar'!"

Mary felt herself fall silent.

"Does that sound like the word of God? If, if somehow this is more than wean's fancies, it's the devil's work, plain and simple. And now what, he wants us to dig him a hole to Hell? Blasphemy, every word, and I won't just stand by and watch anymore."

He drained the remaining beer from the bottle and slammed it down to the counter, "I'll talk with Bowdern," said George, "He will see reason, or I will stop this myself!"

Before Mary could speak the front door creaked open and Big Tom stepped inside. The giant moved towards the kitchen, but George seemed to have no time for either of them. He pushed past them both and left.

She went to pursue but Tom stopped her, "I'll sort 'im out," said the big man, "Get 'im to the pub, ain't nothing cards and whiskey can't sort."

"He's upset," said Mary, "And rightly so. I have to make things right."

With a jutted chin Big Tom pointed up over her shoulder, "More important things," he said, "You'll talk to him come sunup."

Mary turned to find Lilith had disobeyed her again. The girl was sat at the bottom of the staircase, watching. The front door slammed on her back and Mary was left alone with her child. "George should say sorry," said Lilith with a stern face that was beyond her years.

"I told you to go to bed."

"Bad things happen if you're mean to Father Dirt," insisted Lilith, "Very bad things."

Mary sighed, "George shouldn't have blown up like that, but he's not wrong, if something really is speaking to you it's not your dad. This has to stop."

"You're both wrong," said Lilith, "Obey the voice or plague clings to you."

"Who told you that?" Mary asked.

"Father Dirt."

"Don't lie to your mother! Those are Bowdern's words. Has he been speaking with you? Is he telling you what to say?"

Glowering, Lilith shook her head.

"This is not how your father would act," Mary insisted, "I knew him better than anyone, this is not him."

"He says you wouldn't understand at first," said Lilith, "Mumma's too stubborn, that's why he says to me instead."

"Go to your room."

"So, I can show you—"

"Go to your room!"

"Father Dirt misses you Mumma—"

"Room!"

"He wants his wife back."

"Upstairs now!" Mary shouted, "Right now!"

"Wants his wife back." In her mind Mary heard the words repeated, this time in Matthew's voice, spoken from rotten lips with a dead tongue. Visions of the nightmare overwhelmed her. She braced herself against the kitchen table. An uneasy stillness filled the homestead for several heavy heartbeats before Lilith rose to her feet and climbed the stairs. Once her child was out of sight Mary closed her eyes, breathed deeply, and calmed herself as best she could.

I must make things right with George.

She rushed outside. Pillars of dark smoke rose in the distance where the bonfire had stood, and the farm sat in darkness; eerily quiet and still. Down by the front gate she spotted them; two black splotches darker than the darkness that surrounded them. They held a moment at the gate, then started off down the main road towards town.

"George!"

Mary broke into a sprint.

"George!"

Neither man noticed her. They continued along without interruption, not even slowing or turning a head when a straggler from the party stumbled out of the bushes at the edge of the lower paddock and onto the road behind them. The man followed behind and all three gradually faded out of sight.

Mary pushed herself harder, desperate to catch up to the men, when out of nowhere Father Bowdern's words ran through her mind, *"He has chosen to speak to his daughter and not his wife."*

The thought stopped her. Her chest heaved up and down as short sharp breaths came to her. She turned to the dirt, with a new sense of determination.

Discarded bottles and food wrappings surrounded Mary at the base of The Pile. Bouquets suffocated the memorial stone. Roses, carnations, orchids, every flower and every colour, all of them already wilting from the heat. An especially gaudy arrangement had been placed front and centre and hung down over the carved inscription, hiding Matthew's name. She tore the bouquet away and struck it against the ground over and over, spreading a rainbow of broken petals through the weeds and dirt. When all the colour was gone, she dropped the stems and stomped them until they were nothing but a broken green mush.

When calm returned to her, she surveyed the paddock and wider farm from The Pile's base, searching for party stragglers, and dirt followers desperate for some time alone with their messiah. She found no one. *I'm not ruining another dress for this nonsense.*

She began unbuttoning her dress. Her heart hammered, and her hands turned clammy as her fingers fumbled their way up her back. With each noise from the livestock or rustling of leaves she froze in place, scared that someone had snuck up on her. If she was seen, her reputation would be ruined.

When Matthew was alive and the pair snuck out together to make love in the grass beneath the moonlight, she'd cared little for the potential consequences. But with age and loneliness, fear thrived. Questions of why she needed clean dresses anyways filled her mind, her life was dirt and hay, livestock and chores. Tedious. Repetitive. Small. Her world extended the acreage of Faulds Farm and little more.

Hesitating at the last button, Mary contemplated redressing. Giving up her resistance and accepting her lot, her life. *"You've only just started,"* George's words came to her.

With a smile she glanced over each shoulder, seeing no one, she unburdened herself down to her undergarments. The evening breeze washed over her, bathing her in a type of warmth she had not felt for a long while, a warmth that was not intolerable but pleasurable. The night's air caressed her, danced along the parts of her that had to so often be hidden beneath layers of wool and cotton. It rushed through her, each breath feeling like a lover's kiss. She felt like she was back in the corn fields with Matthew, passing the night in each other's embrace, free from the harshness of the world. For a fleeting moment there was peace and serenity. She could've stood there forever.

The tranquillity was broken as she stepped up onto The Pile, she sunk both hands and feet into the dirt and started to climb on all fours like a hound stalking its prey. The taste of stagnant dust smacked across her lips and a tapestry of stains rapidly consumed her body and undergarments as she pushed towards the peak.

Upon making the summit she rose to her feet and stretched out her tightened back. From here all of Faulds Farm could be seen, the broken crops, the homestead, and the barn with its still punctured roof. George had cut the timbers to make the repairs but for the job to be done they would need to drag Big Tom away from his work with the dirt fanatics. At least the weather had held hot, and the farmhands could return to their lodgings instead of being cramped up in the parlour. The hole seemed to almost face her directly; *with some candlelight I could probably see everything inside.*

Neighbouring properties all the way down to Yahl proper could be seen as well. The party had split and migrated downhill, some distant homesteads closer to town were lit by tiny specks of orange and from them muffled sounds of singing, clapping, and cheering wafted up on the quiet country air. She counted nine farms holding celebrations. The fairytale of Father Dirt had spread far and wide and she worried that it may have grown too grand to dismiss.

She drew in a deep breath and sank down to her backside with the exhale, the soft cold dirt felt strangely pleasurable as it cradled the back of her thighs and hindquarters. "Alright," she said softly, "Speak to me then."

Her body tightened. Heart raced. Breathing stopped. Eagerly, she waited to hear her departed's voice once more. A moment passed and then another. Nothing. Nothing but distant crickets chirping.

"Speak to me," she said, a little louder this time, "You wanted me, I'm here."

The night remained still. No voice spoke but her own.

Mary twisted up to her knees and plunged her hands elbow deep into the dirt, raising them back up full of grimy soil, "Is this what you want?" She shouted, "Is it?"

She rubbed dirt across her cheeks and patted some into her ears and hair the way Lilith did. She reached into the dirt again and again, smearing more and more over herself, "Will you talk to me now?" She screamed.

Silence.

She shook her hands as clean as she could and began running them through her hair as she stared wide eyed at the dirt beneath her. "I'm your wife," she whimpered, "You can see storms and gold, but you can't speak to the woman you love?"

Tears welled up in the corners of her eyes, Mary scrunched her face to try and hold them in place, "I've done my best. I kept the farm going, I raised our daughter on my own. I don't know how, but I did that. Did that with no help from you!"

The tears fell and her voice cracked as she shouted to the darkness, "I'm sorry... I tried to get you out of here. I tried to fix the farm. I tried."

She paused a moment, half expecting a response, but no words came. Deep down she knew there would be none but that didn't stop the silence from hurting. There was certainty now; she would never hear Matthew speak again. Being right never felt so joyless.

Dragging herself to her feet, she wiped the muddy tears from her face and started to chuckle, "I knew this was silly, you can't speak, and you can't do anything from where you are. But I hope you can still hear me. I love you Matthew, I'm sorry I let this get so out of hand."

Mary blew a kiss to the night's sky as she slid back down the dirt. She gathered up her clothes and hastily dressed herself.

As she walked back to the homestead part of her wished she had continued after George and not wasted time on such a silly experiment, now she was stuck with cleaning herself and trying to sleep while their issue went unresolved. *It'll be okay,* she reassured herself, *we'll clear the air tomorrow. I'll apologize, and together we can work out a way to stop this Father Dirt nonsense once and for all.*

Chapter Six

Bang! Bang! Bang!

Mary Faulds was jolted awake by a pounding at her bedroom door. From under the door crack there was a flicker of candlelight and a long-twisted shadow that seeped into her chambers. With wild kicks she freed herself from the bedsheets, pulled back the top draw of her side table and gripped Matthew's revolver. "Who's there?"

"Youse gotta hurry," The voice was Big Tom's, "It's Georgie."

She released the gun and wrapped herself in her robe. Out in the hall there was no need for more words, Big Tom's sunken face told her all she needed to know; something was wrong, something serious.

They raced down through the homestead, still groggy with sleep. Tom tore the front door back. Mary expected chaos and terror behind it, but there was nothing of the sort. Faulds Farm was still and calm.

The wind had died while she slept, and silence gripped the property. Above the sky was starless, as black and plain as a widow's veil. It felt as though they had been pulled out of time itself.

They staggered down from the veranda to the warm dirt below. Barefoot they ran. Tom leading the way, and Mary following close behind. As they came down upon the large wooden doors of the barn, Mary could hear screaming coming from inside. "What's happening?" She asked.

"I don't know," said Tom, throwing the barn doors open, "I'm hoping you do."

Inside the air was as still as the grave and as cold as the reaper's touch. A far cry from the warmth of the homestead or the outdoors. All along the rafters magpies sat perched and watching. Their eyes shone like fireflies, a glowing brownish red, the colour of Northern dirt. They stared down at her and Tom, first reminding her of the rats behind the barn the night Lilith ran away, then the birds that flocked to The Pile during the storm, then finally and most strangely, of her mother. Bright but soulless eyes. Mary's blood turned to ice.

"Have they been there long?" She whispered.

"Weren't when I left," said Tom, "Must've flew in through the hole."

That she could've deduced herself. How they got in was of little concern, it was the amount and the speed in which they gathered that uneased her. *A bad omen if nothing else,* Mary thought, *Crows is a murder, but what are magpies?*

The bottom floor of the barn was lined with empty livestock pens, rusted equipment and scattered haybales, further back stood a ladder that reached up to the second half-floor where the men slept. From under the timber slates Mary could see flickering candlelight and a shadow thrashing back and forth violently like prey in a crocodile's jaw. Screams erupted, echoing off the walls, screams of a terror beyond imagining.

"At first I thought he couldn't handle his brown," said Tom, "But he only had two and this don't seem like no drink sickness."

"No, it doesn't," said Mary. "Fetch a doctor, fast as you can."

The giant wasted no time, he broke into a dash and disappeared outside into the darkness.

Mary started up the ladder. With each peg she climbed the bird's heads raised slightly, their eyes fixed on her every move. Sickening thuds rained down from above, the sounds of flesh slamming against wood. It shook the ladder. Halfway up Mary started shaking too, from the banging above or the fear of what awaited her she could not tell.

He needs me, she reminded herself. With sweaty palms and trembling legs, she reached the top and pulled herself up onto the second floor. Before her, George laid drenched in sweat and convulsing atop a bed of mussed straw, flanked on either side by a dwindling reading candle. Mary dropped down beside him and took his hand in hers, "George? What's happening?"

He gave no answer, only an anguished grunt as he ripped his hand from hers and grabbed his stomach.

"George!"

His skin was as pale as the candle wax that dripped beside him and his forehead as hot as the flame. "I'll fetch a cloth and water," Mary said hurriedly.

Half to her feet, a blood curdling cry pulled her back to George. His hardened hands tore into the floorboards beside the bed, breaking his nails and drawing blood. His eyes burned red and welled up in the corners with dark tears. Lumpy veins rose along his sweaty brow and down the side of his strained neck. "Please Lord," George whimpered, his voice came with a bubbly croak as if he was speaking from underwater.

Mary moved in close, "George," she said softly, placing her hands upon him.

He turned to her, but there was no sign of recognition in his eyes. As he stared through her, dirty brown tears started to fall and stain his cheeks. Mary raised a trembling hand to his face and brushed one away, bringing her hand back she saw what was causing the discoloration, dirt. *Did he not wash?*

"Lord..." George sobbed.

He thrashed to one side and began to retch. His body seized up and his eyes bulged out like a bugs. Through a screaming mouth it spewed forth, a black sludge of vomit. It poured down and splattered across the straw and timber, reeking of an open grave. Mary covered her nose and began slapping George's back.

"It— It's okay," said Mary, "Doctor will be here any moment."

She felt his back arch up once again and another clump of black spewed forth. She leaned in close to inspect the slop. *It can't be... Mud?*

"No, no," George murmured.

He twisted his head towards the hole in the side of the roof. "No, no, no."

On hands and knees, he moved towards it, crawling like a dog with a bad hind leg. Mary followed him closely, "Stop," she pleaded, "Please George, don't strain yourself."

He ignored her. He retched again and again, each time more wet dirt churned up and out onto the floor. His lips were coated in mud and grains of dirt were trapped between his teeth. Still, he crawled forwards, his hands and knees slushing in the trail of vomit he left in his wake. Mary remained at his side for each hard-fought inch gained.

A sound like nails down a chalkboard drew her attention. All along the rafters the magpies scurried, their talons scratching into the wooden beams. She followed George and the birds followed her.

"Shoo!" She shouted.

She kicked up the strewn hay around her until she found something, a small trowel. She picked it up and threw it at the magpies.

It clanged against a beam, but none flinched. They stayed watching. *What the—*

Her thought was interrupted by George. "That bastard..."

It was the first time she had heard the man curse. He started to pull himself up by the gnarled edges of the hole. Mary rushed to his side.

The hole was taller and wider than Big Tom. Looking directly outward, The Pile dominated the view, with the homestead and the front gate at the bottom of the trail flanking it on either side.

George was panting heavily, sweating profusely. He glared out at the farm as a chunky froth of dirt sludge seeped through his lips and down the front of his shirt. "Bastard!" He shouted.

Mary wrapped her arms around him, "Stop this," she pleaded, "Lie-down please."

He paid her no mind. He stayed standing, screaming out at the night, as more and more sick continued to flow. Each heave saw the piles grow larger and thicker. The screaming was reduced to a gurgle as mud bubbled up the back of his throat. It did not take long for it to overcome him; it came too fast and too thick. He collapsed into the hay. "George!" Mary cried.

She knelt beside him and rolled him onto her lap. His breathing was laboured, the throw up came now with clumps of compacted dirt. His eyes were glassed over and filled with popped blood vessels.

"George," said Mary, shaking the farmhand, "Stay with me!"

His eyes fluttered a moment, and a look of half recognition came to him, he reached up and grabbed her by her shoulders, he was shaking, and brown bubbles foamed at the corners of his mouth, "Mary," he wheezed.

Mary started to cry, "I'm here," she said.

"Don't trust him."

"Who?" Mary asked.

"Father..."

A deep airless gasp took his words, he clawed at his throat as his skin began to turn blue. Mary pounded on his abdomen, trying to force up the trapped mud, "Breathe George! You have to breathe, please just breathe!"

He gasped and convulsed but did not draw a breath. Mary forced her fingers into his throat to try and clear the blockage, but as soon as she did a new one formed. A few more wretches brought up some splatters of mud, then, in an instant, it stopped. George stopped moving. In through the hole the wind rose from its whisper and the magpies above took flight, out into the darkness.

Mary wiped her hand off against her hips, her nightgown was stained with the tears and vomit of a now silent George. She lowered her ear to his lips and listened, praying to hear even a soft breath, but none came. "George!" Mary shook him, "George!"

There was no response.

A glimpse of light caught her eye, for a moment she thought it was the help she'd sent for, but the light was coming from the wrong direction, it was coming from up at the homestead. Mary looked upon Lilith's window. Her daughter stood at the glass, a burning candle beside her. The light from the flame fell across half her face, splitting her nose down the middle and casting everything to one side in shadow. Mary gripped George's shirt and screamed out at the beacon in the darkness, "You did this!" She cried, "You and your stupid games. Look what you've done!"

Mary slouched back to George; tears fell from her cheeks to his. She clutched his cold face against her chest. His eyes were still open, eyes that had once been so full of kindness and looked upon her with such warmth now stared through her as if she was not even there. She pulled him closer and began to run a hand through his hair as beads of lantern light funnelled through the front gate; help had arrived, but they were too late.

Chapter Seven

Mary Faulds stood at her bedroom window dressed in black. Off in the distance she watched The Pile and the ever-growing pit that sat beside it. The hole was as wide as a wagon and since first breaking ground there had been no less than ten men digging at any one time. Day and night, the work never stopped.

They'd arrived with their picks and shovels before the rising sun on the morning after George's passing. Screams and threats kept them at bay for a short time, but by midafternoon they'd taken over the farm and set to ruining the outer paddock even further.

A whole community sprouted up around The Pile, like weeds in an untended garden. They held a constant vigil around the dirt, prayers and hymns by day, lit candles and mud anointments by night. At noon and sunset Lilith addressed the town from the peak, preaching the so-called word of Father Dirt, all while the more physically capable men of the town toiled in the hole. Buckets of earth were carted up from underground in a steady stream and dumped along edges of the dig site, forming a ring of a dozen small mounds. The offbeat clanging of pick against rock and the hiss of shovels sinking into soil filled the air round the clock. Come evening, it was all Mary could hear. Sleep had already been a struggle, now it was all but impossible.

Faulds Farm and Yahl were at the beck and call of a child. *A child, and a pair of old fools,* Mary reminded herself. It was a sad state of affairs and all she could do was watch. Her only ally was gone and the fire inside her snuffed out. It was her against them all now and she lacked the stomach for a fight.

During the days she wandered about the property like a ghost, aimless and tormented by the past. So much had happened in one summer, the boot prints, the shadow man, the watchful pests, the storm, the gold. *Coincidences and paranoia,* Mary assured herself, *that's all they are. If Matthew won't talk to me, he won't talk to anyone, not even Lilith.*

Of all the thoughts that plagued her, the thoughts of George were the hardest to bare. His teary-eyed face looking up at her begging for help was imprinted on her mind like a photograph on a tintype. It seemed cruel and unjust that good people should die so young and in such horrible ways, Matthew in the landslide and now George in what, to her mind, had to have been some kind of poisoning.

She had pushed hard to get a doctor from the capital city Adelaide to come and perform an autopsy or failing that at least a more senior medical professional from neighbouring Mount Gambier, but her requests were denied. An autopsy was performed, but to Mary's shock they found nothing that constituted foul play. *Liars, I was with him, I saw! Who are they trying to protect?*

When Big Tom returned with help and burst into the barn, they had all seemed eager to get her away and back inside the homestead. At the time this had seemed to be a kindness, to spare her from any further trauma, but as the days rolled on, she grew increasingly unsure. No one wanted to talk about George, and no one would speak of how he died. Unlike the storm and gold, this was not claimed as the work of Father Dirt.

Trying to make sense of that night nearly drove her mad. Awake or asleep, it was all she could think of. She relived the horror a thousand times over. *"Don't trust him. Father..."* A lying priest... *A murdering priest?*

Mary shook the thought from her head. She moved to the mirror, tidied her hair, and examined the black dress she was wearing. It was the same dress she'd worn the day they laid Matthew's memorial stone. The colour had faded since then and the stitching along the hem had grown thin and verged on fraying, but it still fit and that gave her a small sense of happiness, guilty and fleeting as it was. She looked deeply into her reflection; in a way most were too afraid to; worry that the colour in her eyes had faded just as much as the dress came over her. She looked tired and beyond her years. Face swollen. Skin pale. Eyes glassy and eyelids drooped. *I look like I should be the one being put in the ground.*

Retrieving her hat and topcoat, she finished readying her funeral attire. Once properly dressed she went to check on Lilith. They had not spoken much the past few days, Mary had said a short apology after George was taken away, but it had done little good. The girl cared only for Father Dirt and Mary was too grieved and bitter to put effort into mending their bond.

Lilith was still in her sleeping clothes when Mary opened the door, her hair was matted together with clumps of dried out mud and the souls of her feet were as black as coal. The funeral dress Mary had sewn for her laid crumpled on the ground, she picked it up and threw it onto the bed beside Lilith, "Put it on now," Mary demanded.

Lilith did not move; her eyes were fixed out the window on the farm. Mary crossed in front of her and drew the curtains, "Now!"

She reached down and rubbed her daughter's hair between her fingers, flakes of dirt sprinkled down onto Lilith's shoulders, "I'll fetch a washcloth."

"We don't have time for this," Mary insisted as she scrubbed the child, "They'll be laying George to rest soon, this is our last chance to say goodbye."

"They should've buried him here," Lilith grumbled, "Then you wouldn't have to say goodbye, he could talk to us all the time."

Mary pressed the washcloth harder against her daughter, "He wanted to be beside the church."

"Will you be buried here? Next to Father Dirt?"

"I'll be beside you dad," said Mary, "But not here. When this is all over and the town finds a new obsession, I'll get the money to take down The Pile. He'll be down the church one day too."

"No."

"Please stop this," Mary stuffed the girl into the dress and finished cleaning her as best she could, "Don't ruin today."

"Father Dirt belongs here."

But Matthew Faulds doesn't, Mary might've said. Instead, she held her tongue and gave the child the last word in exchange for peace. Taking Lilith's hand, she led her out of the homestead and down the dust sloped path towards the front gate. Halfway down Lilith started tugging at Mary's arm, "I want to go see Father Dirt."

Mary urged her forward, "You can go after," she said, "We have a funeral to attend. You have to pay your respects, it's the least you can do."

The girl fought her for each step, dropping her weight, and kicking and flailing anytime Mary tried to pick her up. As she struggled with the child Mary noticed the spinster making her way up the trail, flanked by a half dozen of her dirt disciples. "Having some trouble dear?" The old woman called out.

"Nothing I can't handle," said Mary.

"I want to see Father Dirt!"

Miss Mackenzie stepped up to the pair and placed a hand on Mary's shoulder, a hand that was quickly shrugged away by the frustrated mother. "Let her be dear," said the old woman, "You can hardly force the poor girl."

"You're not supposed to be here," said Mary, "I told you to stay away after the bonfire."

"Everyone is here," said the spinster, "I understand you've had a challenging couple of days but don't take it out on me. Truly, I am sorry for my behaviour that night, one too many cups of wine I'm afraid."

The old woman and her pack chuckled, but Mary found no humour. "A man's dead," Mary reminded them.

"A tragedy," said the spinster with feigned sympathy, "Truly a tragedy."

The spinster wore a gaudy red dress with mutton sleeves, cinched at the waist, with a lace patterned skirt that rested just above her ankles. *She's dressed like a teenager, the fool.* "I thought you might've forgotten," said Mary, as she looked the spinster up and down. "That's a very bright dress, are you not attending the funeral?"

"No, no," Mackenzie shook her head, "We'll be right along. Though truth be told I never had much to do with your boy. We are just coming to check on the progress before we go."

Mary looked over to the work site in the distance, "They'll be done any day now I imagine. The digging doesn't stop, not even for the dead apparently."

"I want Father Dirt!" Lilith screamed.

"No."

"Let the girl stay. Children deal with grief in their own way, let her be with her father, I'll watch over her and bring her down to you later."

"Neither of you are staying," Mary insisted as she wrestled with Lilith, "We're going."

"No!" Lilith squealed and dug her heels into the ground, "I want to stay!"

As they tussled, Mary noticed more townsfolk making their way up the trail, among them, the Williams couple, Edward and Alice.

"Is everything alright?" Asked Alice.

"Perfect," said Mary as she grappled with the child.

"What's happening?" Asked Edward.

"Lilith wishes to visit Father Dirt," said Miss Mackenzie, "I'm trying to convince Mary here to let me take her up."

"We have the funeral; she can play in the dirt another day."

"We'll watch her," said Alice, "Anything to do our part to help, especially after what happened."

Mary had learnt a long time ago that Mackenzie could not be trusted, but the Williams couple had always been honest and decent people. Alice stepped forward and offered her hand to Lilith, Mary held her child tight. "I want Father Dirt! I want Father Dirt!" Screamed Lilith.

For the longest moment Mary stared at Alice, then the spinster, before finally letting go. Lilith smiled as she took the wife William's hand. "Keep her clean for the funeral," instructed Mary, "She can play around The Pile, but she's not to go on the dirt, and Mackenzie here is to keep her distance."

"Understood," said Alice.

"Funeral is within the hour. It's important Lilith pay her respects."

"Of course," Edward nodded.

Hand in hand Lilith and the William's couple made their way back up the slope, Mackenzie and her entourage followed behind. "Don't worry dear," said the old woman as she passed, "We'll be as good as saints."

Turning her back to them, Mary continued on her way into Yahl proper to the town church. As she approached the large limestone building, she found her eyes drawn not to the tall windows of stained glass or to the elaborate patterned carvings that snaked their way up the walls and along the roof, but rather to the flower beds that lined the church's perimeter. Rows of lavender bushes. Beautiful and blossoming. Somehow, she had never taken notice of them before.

As if summoned by the clicking of her heels against the gravel street top, Father Bowdern stepped out onto the front stoop of the church. His beet red bald spot was visible even from the road and the few clumps of wispy white hair that he held onto stood puffed up like a cockatoo's crest. He raised his hand with a thick grey handkerchief in his grasp and waved, "Mary my dear!"

The old man waddled his way down the flattened earth path, dabbing at his forehead with the cloth every few steps. Mary moved towards him. Her strides were longer and sturdier, and she reached him before he had managed more than a quarter of the pathway.

The priest tucked the handkerchief away in a jacket pocket. "How are you coping my dear?" He asked, as he took Mary's hands in his own. "Dreadfully sorry I could not call upon you after what happened, there's much to attend to these days. The burden of progress has fallen to me and I'm afraid it's rather all consuming."

Despite the heat, the old man's hands were cold and clammy, with small clumps of dirt trapped beneath the fingernails. *Dirty hands for a dirty man.* "I expected no such visit," Mary said, "At least not one of sympathies."

"What do you mean my child?"

"The bonfire." Mary pulled her hands from the father's grip. "You threatened me and George, hours later he passed. The thought crossed my mind that I might be next."

"I did not force the boy to drink," said Father Bowdern.

"Drink?"

"The cause of death. Consumption, no? That's what the doctor told me."

"Mud," Mary snapped. "Mud and dirt."

"My dear, you're in mourning, remember how you were when your husband—"

"I held him as he threw up a stomach full of it. My nightgown still has the stains. He told me he was going to confront you, then he dies. I don't know if it was poison or if he was force feed or what, but I'm not stupid. It was a threat, a message."

"A man of God has no need for threats. Your lad must have taken a wrong turn on his way to my residence, from what I hear he ended up at the public house that evening."

"He didn't stay long."

"Long enough." The priest dabbed his forehead with the kerchief, "If your story were true and the boy died by the dirt, it would be the talk of the town and even further proof of Father Dirt. Would I not have told everyone?"

"Maybe you realised it makes your prophet look more demon than angel."

"Half the town followed Tom up to that barn, are they all lying to you?"

"There wasn't that many—"

"Semantics," Father Bowdern insisted. "I have been patient with you my dear. What's happening up at Faulds Farm must be especially difficult for you, but your defiance grows tiresome. You refuse to see the miracles; you accuse good people of foul play. Anything can be picked apart if you try hard enough, you my child, should stop trying."

"I knew Matthew," Mary's words did as much to remind herself as the priest, "He loved me, he'd talk to me. Something else is happening here and I'm going to figure out who's behind it."

"It'll cost you dearly. We all have our limits, even Father Dirt."

"Matthew," Mary reminded him, "His name was Matthew."

Mary stepped around the father and headed into the church. The air inside was heavy with frankincense and must. Painted saintly portraits adorned the walls and a dozen empty pews lined each side of an aisle that led down to the raised stage at the back of the building. Atop the stage sat George's coffin, a thin pine box, topped with a light spattering of flowers that Mary had picked from around the farm the day prior. Next to it stood the priest's pulpit, ornately carved from a single piece of maple with a golden cross affixed to the front. Mary could not help but compare the coffin to the podium. It seemed unjust to her that the Lord should require such opulence while good men were made to lie to rest in meagre conditions.

She took a seat in the front row. As she waited for the service to start, fear and doubt crept into Mary's mind. Fear that too much time spent living in the past had blinded her to the present. That perhaps it was all as Bowdern had said, the miracles were real, and Matthew was back. Perhaps the life she had known was not as it seemed. Maybe their love was one sided. Maybe Matthew did not speak to her because he did not care.

"Don't trust him. Father..."

George may have meant Father Dirt. Maybe Matthew was the murderer, and Father Bowdern had simply stepped in to cover it up and preserve his saintly reputation. There had been barely enough time to celebrate an anniversary before Matthew's passing, how well can one truly know a man in such a short period of time? It occurred to her, that George and Matthew both thought of her as a good and kind woman, but she was not without her moments of anger. If a rage took her and she was beyond the reach of consequences as the dead are, how would she react? *Matthew was a good man,* she insisted to herself, *Father Dirt is a lie.*

She was stressed and lacking in sleep. Surrounded by lunatics for so long that she was becoming one. *The first thought is usually the right one.* It was all one big game, started by Lilith and increasingly taken over by the rest of the town, Bowdern and Mackenzie more so than anyone. George's words came to her again, *"Don't trust him. Father..." I won't.*

She felt sick at the idea that George's killer might be the one to oversee his burial, but the farmhand made his wishes to rest beside a church known in the past and Mary was not going to deny them. *A church is a church, even if a monster dwells within.*

Time ticked by slowly and the pews remained empty. Footfall at the back of the church filled her with hope, but upon turning she saw it was only Father Bowdern. The old man shuffled into the church, easing the door shut behind him. "We'd best be getting on," he said.

Mary stood up, "There's no one here."

"I know, but that does not seem likely to change. Everyone is busy after all, there's lots of work to be done up at your farm."

"A man is dead."

"I'm sure they will visit the grave, there is only so much light to dig in."

Mary sunk back down onto the hard wooden bench defeated. She picked at the sleeve of her dress, pulling up thread and skin alike. "Lilith is meant to be here, the Williams' promised they'd be along."

"A harmless mistake I'm sure," said Father Bowdern, "I wouldn't worry."

There are no mistakes when Mackenzie is skulking around. The priest approached the pulpit and with little fanfare began the proceedings. He sprinkled a few small spattering's of holy water over the coffin and read only one psalm before calling upon Mary for the eulogy.

From behind the polished wood of the pulpit she looked out into the rows of empty pews and sighed. Her eyes watered but no tears fell. Words came slow but steady as she began. A speech meant for a hundred heard by no one but a half-asleep priest. "I'm not a good public speaker," Mary started, "But I suppose that won't matter much today..."

She spoke at length of George's kindness and good nature, about the good times they shared and how even during the bad times he managed to make her smile, how with him around everything seemed like it was going to be okay.

"There aren't many I've loved in my time," she said, drawing her speech to a close, "My father, my husband, my daughter... And you. I'm sorry I never told you while you were here. Four people and I fear I've lost them all. Twenty-four is too young for this much loss, I can't stomach much more, you might just be my last love. With all my heart I hope you are at peace, and I pray we'll be reunited someday. I still want to know how you did that magic trick."

Mary chuckled slightly to herself, "There's not a day you won't be missed, and I'll see your grave is properly tended to, I won't let grief keep me away like it did with Matthew. Goodbye George."

Mary walked over to George and planted a kiss on his coffin. Father Bowdern clapped a hand against his knee as he rose to his feet, "Well said, well said indeed my dear."

Mary said nothing. *It should be him in that box, not George.* Avoiding the father's gaze, Mary looked out to the still empty pews, "There are no pallbearers. How are we getting George to his plot?"

"It is rather unfortunate," said Father Bowdern, "But I'm afraid we have no choice but to retire and arrange some men for another day."

"Nonsense," said Mary, bracing the side of the coffin, "We can try ourselves."

The old man hunched himself over and began rubbing the lower back of his jacket, "Bad back I'm afraid."

"Of course."

Realising her grip, Mary's eyes held on George for a moment. She had failed to bury her husband in the church's graveyard, she would not allow the same fate twice. George would be laid to rest that day, no matter what was required to do so.

She stormed off down the aisle. "Don't leave," she instructed Father Bowdern as she passed.

"Where are you going?"

"To find some men with sturdier backs."

Outside the streets were empty, not a man or horse in sight. Yahl had become a ghost town. Shouts for assistance went unanswered and a search on foot of the nearby stores and lanes turned up nothing. Irritated, Mary decided to make for the only place in town guaranteed to still draw a crowd, the pub.

The public house was the first building the town's settlers built, before houses and churches, the watering hole stood. Old and wide, and standing at two stories tall, it consumed an entire street corner. To most it was considered the unofficial town centre.

Inside the air was thick, heavy with tobacco smoke and body odour that groped at the skin and insulted the nostrils. The pub appeared to have been a grand place once but had long since fallen into decay and disrepair. The hardwood floors, the intricately carved skirtings. They must have been a marvel when the place opened, but now, they were as sticky as treacle, with chipped chunks missing and poorly cleaned stains of blood, vomit, and urine scattered throughout. From beneath the broken floor panels, a black roach the colour of death scurried up and off behind the long wrap around bar that sat at the room's centre.

A stocky barman manned the counter, wiping down dirty glasses with an even dirtier rag. He noticed the pest and stomped it but made no effort to clean the splatter. *So, this is where Tom goes. Where George went on his last night... Did they slip something into his drink here?*

Little more than a half dozen patrons took up stools, most had already succumbed to drink and laid face down in puddles of beer and drool. Each man she saw made her more uncomfortable than the last. They were dirty and not from a hard day's work in the field. Still, she would not be deterred and moved towards the bar.

The barman cocked his head up, slammed down the glass he was cleaning and pointed back to the door. "Oi!" He shouted, "You mad woman? Back outside before I have the law on ya, men only."

"If you can't stand to piss, you can't sit to drink," cackled one of the barflies.

"Go fetch them," Mary told the barman, "I'll be gone before you make it back."

The barman grumbled and poured himself a large shot of whiskey.

Mary had come in search of capable men and in that regard, was severely disappointed. Only two patrons seemed to have any life in them, a pair of labourers with weathered faces but able bodies. She produced her coin purse and began rummaging through it as she approached. "I've come from a funeral down the road," she told them, "We're in need of pallbearers, I'll give you two shillings a piece."

The younger of the two men struck a match against the bar top and lit a poorly rolled cigarette, "What's a couple shillings gonna be worth next week?" He asked, "Haven't you heard Father Dirt's about to make us rich?"

Mary sighed. *It's not just the church, even the drunks have fallen to madness.* Her eyes fluttered for a moment as she tried to keep a pleasing face, "Two shillings will buy you enough beer to see you through the evening."

The older of the two turned to face her, "A pound a piece would see us through the week," he grinned, revealing a set of blackened, mismatched teeth that sent a chill up Mary's spine. *I thought Tom had it bad.*

She returned to her purse in search of coin she knew she did not have. The younger man knocked against the bar top as he ashed his cigarette into a nearby tray. "Well?" He asked, "We got a deal?"

"A pound each is unreasonable."

"Walk on then."

Mary slammed her purse upside down against the counter, cupping a hand against its side so coin would not spill everywhere. Pulling the purse back revealed a small pile of mostly bronze; pennies and three pence. "This is all I have."

The two men shared a look and a hidden whisper. The younger rested his smoke on the corner of the tray and began scrapping the coins along the bar as he mumbled a count to himself. The older continued to drink, glancing over periodically to check on the progress.

"A pound and a florin," said the younger as he lifted his cigarette back to his lips for a long puff.

The men shared another private look, much to Mary's annoyance. The tavern had been stirred awake by her arrival. All the patrons stared, and none made any effort to hide it. *Nothing cures a hangover like the presence of a woman,* Mary thought to herself. Yahl was deserted, everyone who wasn't here was up at Faulds Farm. She was alone with a gang of bitter men, half of whom started at her out of lust and the other out of disdain, which group frightened her more she could not decide. Mary needed to leave now. "Do we have an accord then?" She asked, trying to prod them along.

They turned back to face her. The elder drank the last of his beer and spoke, "You're lucky we can't say no to a pretty face."

A lopsided rotten grin stretched out across the man's face. Mary did her best to not show any of the disgust she felt at the sight of it. "Hurry along then," she said, making for the exit as quick and calm as she could.

The men rose from their stools with little enthusiasm and followed her out, whistles and insults bellowed out from the other barflies as they passed.

As the trio walked the empty main street back to the church the younger man managed to smoke his way through three fresh cigarettes, all whilst making a pitiful attempt at flirting with Mary. The older hung further back, counting the payment aloud and insisting over and over that they were good people for coming down from their original price.

Back at the church they found Father Bowdern lounging in the front row ruffling through a newspaper. Mary walked right past the priest and up to George's side. She stroked the coffin gently, "Sorry," she whispered, "You deserved better."

The young man strode up behind her and cleared his throat with a phlegmy cough, "This it?"

"Show some respect," Mary said sternly, "And care. Drop him and they'll bury you next."

The man raised his palms and chuckled, "Mercy," he said through a smug smile.

The hired hands took positions on either side of the coffin and with deep grunts lifted George into the air. Mary braced the centre and together they moved down the aisle and outside to the adjoining graveyard.

George's grave had been dug at the far end, up against a set of rusted over gates. Far from scenic, but practical and affordable. The procession moved him along slowly. Mary's forearms burned under the strain of the weight, but she was determined not to let George fall. Father Bowdern followed behind, issuing half-hearted words of encouragement that proved more annoyance than inspiration.

At the grave's edge they lowered the coffin down beside the mound of dirt that waited to entomb it. The men tried to flee as soon as the wood touched the ground, but Mary had none of it and insisted they help lower George in as well. With groans and rolled eyes, the drunks agreed.

Father Bowdern stumbled through the Lord's Prayer as the coffin was lowered into the earth, splashing the lid with holy water as he spoke. Mary was struck by the realization that after this George would be truly gone. Memories of the man flooded her mind. All the laughs they'd shared, the evenings spent confiding in one another, the hopes and dreams they'd had for the future, the feeling of his hand in hers as they danced on his final night.

The thud of the coffin hitting six feet pulled her from the haze and she found herself absentmindedly scratching at the back of her hand. Blood pooled up and ran down to her wrist. She quickly wiped it away, praying no one had seen and clasped the damaged hand with her other to try and hide what had happened.

Looking to ensure the attention was not on her Mary noticed there was no ditch digger present. "Where's the digger?" She asked.

"Running a little late it seems," said Father Bowdern, "He was spending the morning working up at Faulds Farm, but he assured me he'd be back in time for the burial."

The funeral had started late, and Mary had wasted no small amount of time finding pallbearers, it was clear to her that just like Lilith, Mackenzie and the William's, the digger was not going to show. "You'll have to do it," said Mary to the barflies, "Please?"

"Fat chance," said the older drunk, "We don't work for free."

"You barely worked for money," said Mary, "I gave you a half weeks wages for five minutes, could you not do a simple kindness?"

"Deal's a deal," said the younger, "And we've got coin to spend."

The young drunk leant in close, he reeked of beer and smoke. "When you're through with all this though," he said, "You should come back down the pub, we'll shout you a drink, treat you right."

I should smack him, make his teeth match his ugly friends. "I'd rather lay down in that hole than spend another unnecessary minute in your company."

The older drunk threw his head back in laughter and with a wrapped arm around the younger's shoulder led him away, Mary and Father Bowdern were left alone once more. Without hesitation the priest returned to rubbing his lower back and feigning injury. "I'll do it," said Mary as she clawed off her topcoat, "I'll do everything."

The old man said nothing, just stood and stared. Mary stormed off to fetch a shovel. The only one she could find was in the church's back shed, it had a warped and rusted blade and a splinter ridden handle, *all the good ones are up at Faulds Farm no doubt.*

With forceful strokes she stabbed at the mound beside the grave with the broken spade, raising small piles up and tossing them down. As the hole gradually filled her hands grew red with splinter punctures and bubbling blisters that sat just beneath the skin, waiting to rise.

Sweat fell from her brow. Her lower back tightened. The smell of churned earth filled her nostrils with each heavy breath she sucked in. Progress was slow and hard earned, but Mary was determined.

In time the dirt dwindled, the grave filled, and the coffin disappeared out of sight. *He's truly gone now,* Mary thought. A lump rose up the back of her throat and for a moment she thought she might cry, but no tears fell, and she soldiered on shovelling.

Only a couple feet remained when her shovel slipped through a shallow part of the mound and struck the solid ground beneath. Her elbows popped, and a sharp pain rippled up her arms and through her bones. She dropped the spade. Tears finally came, accompanied by a lengthy scream, "For God's sake!"

The curse bounced off the nearby headstones and echoed back to her. Father Bowdern looked as though his heart was about to give out. He dropped the remaining holy water and his kerchief, "This is sacred ground," he barked, "Control yourself."

Mary ripped off her hat along with a small clump of hair and slammed it against a nearby headstone, "Damn it! God damn it!"

The old priest was lost for words. Mary dropped to her knees and with bare hands pushed the remaining dirt into the grave. Tears streamed down into the hole alongside the earth. She felt the old man slowly back away. By the time the hole was filled, Mary Faulds was alone and out of tears.

Chapter Eight

Mary Faulds rose from the side of the grave, her hands and knees caked in dirt, muddy tears streaking down the sides of her face. She closed her eyes and inhaled deeply, holding the breath a moment before releasing it. With the exhale her eyes fluttered open and fixed on George's tombstone. Tenderly she brushed the monument. "Goodbye," she said, "I'm going to fix this, I promise."

With the back of her hand she wiped her sniffling nose, "You were a good man, I'll see you have your justice."

Mary left the graveyard with her head high, and her purpose assured. Her body and clothing were dishevelled and dirty, but inside she felt clean and calm.

Arriving home she approached the front gate, raised the rope coil that fastened it in place and threw it open. She strode through and up the trail towards the homestead, not bothering to shut the gate behind her. *It'll only slow them down.*

Over in the outer paddock there were too many people to count. A wall of men, half-dressed and covered in filth, stretched out around the dig site, blocking out any view of the hole they were working on. A few young women walked between them, handing out food and refreshments. If any man spoke their words could not be heard, only the steady clanking rhythm of pickaxes striking the earth.

A smaller group, cleaner and properly dressed, were massed further up at the base of The Pile. They stood in silent vigil, waiting for word from above where Lilith dance about. The Williams were nowhere in sight. *No one can be trusted. The Williams, Mackenzie, Bowdern, I should put the lot of them in that hole they're so obsessed with.*

The crisp crunch of dirt beneath Mary's shoes gave way to drawn out creaks as she stepped up onto the veranda. She threw the front door open. The hinges rattled and the handle slammed into the drywall, leaving a sugar dusting of shattered plaster to trickle down to the hardwood. Moving to the stairs Mary heard the sound of clinking glass coming from the kitchen, followed by an all too chipper call, "You're back," cried the spinster, "I was just fixing some refreshments for Lilith and the boys."

Mary paid the old woman no mind and climbed the staircase to her bedroom without a word. She went straight to the nightstand, unlocked the draw, and pulled out Matthew's pistol. A flick of the wrist rolled out the cylinder. Fully loaded, just as she had left it. Mary let out a short chuckle.

When she came back downstairs, an uncharacteristically nervous Miss Mackenzie was waiting for her. The woman was fidgeting with the cuffs of her sleeves and seemed unable to decide if she should look at Mary or not. Stepping down to the ground floor, the spinster moved to meet her. "Are you okay dear? You look a bit of a mess, maybe we should get you cleaned—"

Mary collided shoulder to shoulder with the old woman, knocking the senior down to the floorboards. She landed on her rear with a heavy thud, but quickly rolled over onto hands and knees. Mary stood over her. She cocked the hammer to the pistol but kept the gun low. "Get off my property. You step foot on my farm again and that hole out there becomes your grave."

The old bag said nothing, only whimpered like a scolded dog. Mary walked on outside. As she moved down the front yard slope and across the upper paddocks she took long measured breaths, as if she was already in her firing stance, ready to pull the trigger.

She kicked the gate to the outer paddock open. Curious heads turned, and a few townsfolk started moving towards her with waving hands and joyful greetings. When she twisted her arm out to show the gun, they all stopped.

"Tools down," she shouted, "Right now!"

Those circled about the hole dropped their shovels and picks, and raised their hands, but down in the hole the echoed sounds of breaking stone and shifting earth continued to call out.

"I said tools down!"

Everyone above ground started pleading for the others to stop their work. Mary looked to The Pile, to her daughter. "Inside Lilith," she called, "Room, right now."

"No," the five-year-old shouted back, "I'm not going!"

Lilith still wore the black dress that Mary had sacrificed so much sleep to sew, but it was ruined beyond repair, torn to tatters and smeared in dirt.

"Now," Mary insisted, "I'm your mother!"

Movement around the base of The Pile caught Mary's attention, from out the crowd Edward and Alice Williams stepped forward. "We're so sorry," called out Alice, edging towards her, "But how can you say no to that face?"

"We'll reimburse you for the dress," added Edward, "Let's just calm down, whatever this is—"

"Don't tell me to calm down! A man is dead, and you all show no decency. Instead of paying respects you waste your day destroying my land, turning my daughter against me! You should be ashamed of yourselves, of what you've become."

From out the crater Big Tom's head emerged, his cheeks crusted with more dirt than her own and a confused expression on his face. He pulled himself up out of the hole. "Bloody hell Mary, put that down."

The big man's presence seemed to embolden the mass. They started creeping towards her with raised hands and soft voices, like she was a child throwing a tantrum. Mary raised the revolver up over her head, barrel aimed square at the heavens. "You're trespassing," she told them, "Leave or I'll shoot."

They did not stop. They continued closing in, their chorus of pleas growing ever louder. Big Tom's gruff voice stood out amongst them, "Careful now," he said, "Ain't no good in using that."

Mary's fortitude started to waver. Her muscles tightened and trembled, "Leave and I won't have to."

"Father Dirt wants them here," Lilith cried from above. "Faulds Farm is for everyone!"

Some close to The Pile sought refuge behind the dirt, but most of the town were rallied by the little girl's words. The pleas for her to calm turned bitter.

"This is Father Dirt's land, not yours!"

"She wants the gold for herself."

Mary's chest tightened and breaths came quick and shallow as the mob closed in.

"Just put it down," urged Big Tom, "Nice 'n easy."

Sweaty palms turned the dirt on Mary's hands to mud.

"Drop it," ordered Edward, "You don't want this."

"Relax Mary, relax," said Alice.

They're not going to leave. Mary started shaking, but not from fear. "I said now!" She screamed and squeezed the trigger.

The shot rang out like a thunderclap. Burnt gunpowder filled the air. Her arm twitched with the recoil, but she kept the gun high. Everyone was silent. Everyone was frozen.

Mary knew now was the time to press her point, but could not manage a word, no one could. For a dozen heartbeats Fauld's Farm was as still and quiet as stone. Then, a shrill voice from behind her broke the silence, "Disarm her!" Cried the spinster, "Now you cowards, now."

Eyes fluttered as if awaking from a dream, faces of disbelief turned to faces of anger and determination. In an instant they were upon her. Hands grabbed from every direction, pulling at her dress and hair. Boots trod on her toes and shouting filled her ears. Mary moved as best she could, throwing elbows, kicking the shins. She kept the gun raised and waved it about as much as possible so that it would be hard to take from her. Cocking the hammer back, she prepared to fire another warning shot just as a large grubby hand grabbed her wrist and yanked her forward. A half dozen wrestling townspeople were knocked to the ground as she was pulled in close to Big Tom. The giant held her at the wrist with one hand and the bicep with the other, "Drop it Mary."

Mary tried to squirm free, but his grip was like a vice. "Tom, please."

"Give it. Don't be disrespecting Father Dirt like this."

Through her wild dirt-streaked hair Mary looked up at the man who was supposed to be her husband's best friend. The man who had helped build Faulds Farm into what it was. The man who had turned his back on her and her beloved. "Traitor," she hissed. "To Hell with you."

The big man sighed, "Sorry."

He squeezed her tighter. His face scrunched up and with a grunt he forced her forearm back against the joint. Her arm bent until it could take no more. There was a sickening pop and snap, then a bang.

Her arm broke and the revolver fired. A jagged lump of bone pierced the creased skin of Mary's inner elbow. Her arm faced the wrong way, and her fingers lost all feeling. She dropped the gun and screamed, but not as loud as the spinster.

"She tried to kill me!" the old woman cried, "She tried to kill me!"

The giant dragged Mary to the ground. Several rushed the pistol and took it away. With her face in the weeds, she turned to see the Miss Mackenzie on the ground again, this time on her back with a spout of blood gushing out from above her kneecap. The crimson poured out of a still smoking hole in her dress and dribbled down her leg to the ground. The dirt eagerly drank the blood as the spinster turned as pale as curdled milk. Mackenzie's faithful rushed to her side, compressing her leg with their shirts and overcoats, and holding her hands and stroking her hair for comfort. It did her little good. The old bag howled like a cow giving birth.

"Fetch the law," someone shouted.

Mary tried to get to her feet, but Tom kept her pinned to the dirt as everyone waited for the constable to arrive. Tears stained her cheeks and the pain in her shattered elbow grew worse and worse with each passing moment. For a shot of morphine, she would have been more than happy to deal with the law.

The wait was long, but how long Mary could not say. She was trapped in a waking nightmare, her body in agony, her mind in turmoil. Fear was the prevailing feeling, fear for what this would mean for her and her daughter. *If she bleeds out, I might never see Lilith again.*

Cries for her daughter went unanswered. With the town gathered and gabbing all around her she could hear little and see even less. *Please be safe,* Mary thought, *be safe and know that I love you.*

As time wore on the townsfolk grew increasingly agitated, screaming threats and throwing rocks as Mary laid helpless, unable to defend herself. Big Tom had betrayed her, but he was not evil,

"Whoever throws the next stone gets they teeth smashed in with it!" He shouted.

After that no one dared to even look at her for too long.

When the constable finally arrived, he granted her a small mercy by not forcing cuffs on her, but he was far from gentle. He shoved in the back every few steps as they made their way down the trail to his wagon, demanding she move faster. The crowd followed them closely.

As Mary sat hunched over in the back of the wagon cradling her broken arm, she looked out on all their faces. Hate or indifference, none showed sympathy. Behind the mob, further up the slope, Mackenzie had been raised onto a chair and was being given medical attention. It was there that Mary finally caught sight of her daughter again, she was at the old woman's side, holding her hand. Fresh tears welled up in Mary's eyes, "Lilith!"

Her little girl looked over, but her gaze did not linger long. There was no chance for Mary to say more, the constable put the whip to the horses, and they were off. She watched as the dirtied faces of those who had stolen her home slowly faded away. She watched her daughter disappear. Faulds Farm disappear. The Pile disappear.

The ride down to the police station was long and filled with potholes, each bump in the road brought fresh pain to the break in her arm. When they arrived at the station, she was placed into one of the two barred cells the town had, fortunately the one next to her was empty. *At least there'll be quiet.*

The cell was small, a glorified cupboard of exposed concrete, barely large enough for the tiny bed cot and poorly cleaned chamber pot within. Hours passed waiting for medical attention, but none surfaced. Instead of a doctor and morphine she was given a scrap of cloth to sling her arm, some whiskey to numb the pain and a needle and fishing line to sew her wounds.

She took a deep swig from the whiskey bottle, "I need a doctor, right now."

Constable Dunne reached through the bars and snatched the bottle from her, "No can do," he smirked as he indulged in the spirit himself, "Doctor's busy tending to poor Mackenzie. We'll see how you shake out. If you don't improve, I'll fetch him."

You'd need even more misguided faith than those fools up at The Pile to think this'll improve, Mary thought as she tried her best to sling her arm. The elbow had turned a sickly pus yellow, and pieces of misplaced bone poked up from under her skin in all directions.

"Will she live?" Mary asked.

"Surprised you give a damn."

Mary despised the woman but did not wish her dead, especially now that her fate relied so heavily on her living. *If she survives it's hard labour, if she doesn't it's the noose.*

"It was an accident," Mary insisted, "We bump heads from time to time, but I'd never harm her."

"Don't need to convince me none." He took another drink from the bottle and looked her up and down, "Doc reckons she'll pull through just fine. Probably gonna have a limp from now on, but he ain't worried about her dropping just yet."

"And Lilith?" Mary asked, "What'll happen to her?"

"Funny you should ask." A toothy smile peered out from under the constable's bushy moustache, "The little angel insisted on staying with Miss Mackenzie and even after everything Mackenzie's offered to take the girl in."

"You gave my daughter to the woman I shot?"

Dunne chuckled. "It ain't rightly regular that's for sure, but I don't intend on being the one to go against Father Dirt's progeny, look how that turned out for you. Besides the Williams' and some of the other townsfolk have made plans to stop in and lend a hand, seeing as she'll be in recovery and all."

Mary tried her best to convince herself this was good news. Lilith could have been sent away to an orphanage and lost to her forever, at least this way she knew where her girl was. Regardless, her blood still boiled at the thought of the old woman poisoning her daughter's mind even further.

The constable stayed until sunset, then Mary was left on her own, locked in a cage in the dark. She laid on her bed cot and thought about how wrong the day had gone; how wrong everything had gone in just a few weeks.

Chapter Nine

A stab of pain jolted Mary Faulds awake. She lurched upright, the rusted springs and hinges of her cot squealing as she rose. On instinct Mary reached for her swollen elbow, it was sore and numb to the touch, but not what woke her. There was a tightness in the small of her back. An aching like that of a rotted tooth biting into toffee. *I'll be hunched like Mackenzie if I'm forced to stay here,* Mary thought as she did her best to stretch out.

The cell was as black as a crow's feathers and as quiet as a crypt. Mary could not tell the hour, late evening, early morning, it was impossible to say. Time moved differently behind bars.

She rolled to her side and with her good arm massaged the tender muscle until the worst of the pain had left her. For several heartbeats there was peace. Her body started to relax, and her eyes grew heavy again with sleep. But, before a dream could take her, the pain returned, this time in her abdomen. It was tight and tense, an unrelenting constant ache.

She curled up like a millipede, biting into her pillow and gripping the sheets. Groaning and cursing, as never-ending minute after never-ending minute dragged on. Just when she thought she could take no more, the pain finally broke again and subsided into a dull throb. *Did I wet myself?*

Slowly, Mary slid a hand up under her skirt and between her legs. Her inner thighs were smeared with a cold, strangely coarse wetness that led all the way up to her privates. *Of course it happens now.* Pulling her hand back, she expected to see blood, instead, she found the tips of her fingers coated with a thick brown sludge. *This early?*

Dunne had left her poorly provisioned and without candles, her only light came from the dim waxy glow of the moon that bled in through the small, grated window behind her bed. She twisted her hand beneath it, desperate for a clearer view. *No, it can't be.*

Mud. Fresh and slimy, with the stench of damp earth. All the blood left her face. She grew lightheaded. Dizzy. Her heart thumped slow and heavy. Breathes were hard come by. "No," the word fell from her lips, "No, no, no."

She looked around for help. "Dunne?" She cried, "Dunne? Someone? Anyone?"

She pounded the side of her fist against the iron bars, "Someone help me! Please!"

Nothing. No one. She was alone.

Another cramp gripped her. Mary's knees buckled, and she let out a primal scream. There was a stirring inside her, a mass moving down through her nether region, a monstrous clot. She tore back her skirt, terrified of what she would see, but needing to know. Clumps of mud were spread across her inner thighs and droplets of dirty water ran down her leg and onto her feet, tickling her along the way.

It was agony as the mass neared breaching. Worries that she might faint and break another bone against the concrete floor filled her mind. *Please stop, please make it stop.*

Memories of Lilith's birth rushed back to her, all that pain and suffering, condensed to a single moment. With labour there had been joy waiting for her at the end, her baby girl. There would be no such happiness this time.

Her abdomen tensed as the clot started to force its way out of her. Water the colour of outhouse run off dribbled down from between her legs. She screamed as the glob of dirt seeped out from her sex, sleek and slimy, like a hacked-up ball of phlegm. Brown and soggy, the colour and consistency of chewed up tobacco. It spread out between her legs and down her thighs, filling the cell with the unmistakeable stench of death.

Get out of me! With gritted teeth she pushed. The pressure in her abdomen was unbearable. A tight squeezing, like an old dish cloth being wrung out. Agony without end.

You've given birth, she reminded herself, *you can handle this.* With all she had she pushed again. A flash of heat shot through her pelvis and the mudpie was free. It splattered against the floor with a wet thud, spraying her legs and feet, spreading muck up her skirt and between her toes.

Her stained legs brought back memories of the nightmare. *Father Dirt wants his wife back,* the words came to her in both Matthew's and Lilith's voices, spoken in unison. *It's all real. This is how he gets me back?*

The dirty flow secreting from between her legs grew thicker and heavier with each passing moment. Veins all across her body raised up from under the skin, thick and bubbled, dark as tree bark. All her blood was turning, not just what came from between her legs.

Mary Faulds now knew how she was going to die. She would share the same fate as George. A scream, a clenched fist. Mary split her knuckles against the cell door. Lilith and Bowdern were right, Matthew had returned to Yahl. *But he loved me, how could he?*

For a dozen heartbeats there was only terror. More and more cold clots oozed out of her and cramps as sharp as razors kept her hunched over. *No, it's fine, everything's fine,* she told herself, *just clean yourself up and you'll be fine.*

There were no towels or rags for the mess. Nothing to fashion a sanitary liner from. The only scrap of cloth she had was being used to hold her arm in place. Out of desperation she grabbed the bed sheet, bit down on a corner and with her good arm tore it into swatches. She scrubbed her legs and sex, desperate to be clean, desperate to wake up and this all be a horrible dream.

When the mud kept coming faster and heavier, she stuffed the ripped-up bedding between her legs and pressed it tight. Still, she felt the wetness growing, soaking through the cotton. The fear and uncertainty of what was happening to her body reminded Mary of her first period. Mother never prepared her for the hardships of womanhood. When she first found those red spots inside her bloomers, Mary thought she was being punished for some forgotten sin. Everything she did was a sin according to her mother and if she had taken anything away from Sunday sermons it was that God loved punishing women for any fault he could, real or imagined.

It took two full years before she had the courage to tell another soul about the bleeding. *Who'll help Lilith?* The thought of her daughter suffering through the same shame and confusion she had brought Mary to tears. *There's so much I haven't told her, so much I'm going to miss.*

Tears ran down her cheeks, mud down her legs. Mary pressed the tattered sheets against herself even tighter, hoping foolishly to clot the leaking. There was nothing to be done, nothing but wait. More and more dirt poured from her, and with it came more and more pain. Her chest grew tighter, breathes shorter. She felt as though she were trapped in a screw press, pinned on both sides, all air and life being squeezed from her.

Half thoughts raced through her mind, of Matthew, of George, of Lilith's life without her, all the things she would miss, all the things she should have done different. It was too much. Mary staggered back towards the cot, lightheaded and dizzy. The cell grew blurry, then black.

"God's nails!"

Mary awoke to the constable yelling. She was sprawled out, half hanging off the bed. Thin beams of sunlight streamed in from the grate, bathing the cell in warm honey coloured light.

"Who raised you?" The constable shouted.

Still half-asleep Mary craned her head upward, from beyond the bars Dunne rushed about crossing his chest, his face turned away from her. He stepped out of sight a moment. When he returned, he held a small wooden bucket of soapy water and a sponge. "You don't eat til this place is spotless," he told her.

"Doctor," Mary whimpered, "Please I need—"

"Doctor's busy, your arms the same as yesterday."

"No, for the..." Mary pointed to the middle of the cell where the mud had fallen.

Instead of a dark brown clump of dirt she saw a stain of crimson. *Blood?* Between her legs the scrunched sheets had changed too, red splotches all over. The only sign of dirt throughout the cell was on Mary's body and beneath her fingernails, remnants from George's grave the day before.

"I'm not an idiot," the constable insisted, "I know about women's monthlies, you'll be fine. I'll fetch you some rags and fresh linens, but when I get back this best be all cleaned and taken care of."

Mary barely heard the man. She studied the sheets. Confused, scared, relieved.

"You understand?" Dunne asked.

"Yes, I do..."

The constable left and Mary sat at the edge of her cot for the longest time, reliving the night before, trying without luck to make sense of what had happened.

Chapter Ten

Mary Faulds awoke to the sound of a Billy club rattling against the bars of her cell. Three uneasy nights had passed since she was detained. Her first morning had started with curses and chores, shame and embarrassment. The rest had been easier and each the same, the constable banging against the iron and a stale breakfast. Today however, the lawman came without a food tray.

Mary rose slowly, her neck stiff and sore, and rested on her good elbow. Her mattress was paper-thin, and the springs of the bed cot dug into her as she sat up. The discomfort was a welcome distraction from her bad elbow, a new pain was almost as good as none. Despite persistent requests, a doctor had yet to see her. Her only relief from the pain was the occasional mouthful of liquor when the constable felt generous.

The elbow had swollen to nearly double the size of her good one. It was red and hot to the touch, with blotched patches of yellow discolouration throughout, pus pockets. If she was lucky, she would get to keep her arm; she did not feel lucky.

At least the cramps have died down, she thought. Each time she checked the rag in her undergarments her heart skipped a beat, unsure if mud or blood awaited her. It was only ever blood.

She'd been a fool. She was certain she'd seen it plain, her monthly and George's death, washed the mud from her gown and hands near a dozen times before she felt clean again. But blood stained the concrete not mud, and at the funeral when the priest told her it was sick that took George, he had at long last told her some truth.

Perhaps her mind was slipping away, but the only proof of Matthew's return left with it. Father Dirt or not, the rains eventually fall. Father Dirt or not, men will give gold for influence. Most men of Yahl lacked means, but an institution, one rich and old, could burden the cost. Bury the wealth in the night, dig it up in the morning. Now more than ever she knew it was all a lie.

The constable struck the bars again, "Up ya get."

Mary rubbed the sleep from her eyes, "No breakfast?"

The lawman unfastened a ring of brass keys from his belt, flicked through several before settling on one and sliding it into her cell door. The lock clicked twice, and the door swung open. "You're getting out today."

Mary rushed to her feet and a sharp pain rushed to the break in her arm. She staggered a moment, catching herself against the cell door. Black splotches like mud filled her vision. "How? I haven't had a trial or anything."

"They finished digging yesterday, Father Dirt calls your name."

"Matthew. His name was Matthew."

"Call him what you like, either way he's asking for you. There's to be a celebration come midday and I've been told it can't go ahead without the wife."

"You've let me rot for three days." Mary pulled herself back from the cell door, stood firm and looked the lawman dead in his eyes, "No pity, no care. Now all that changes on the command of a child?"

"A child who speaks for Father Dirt."

Mary spat at the man's feet. "Lock it back up and leave me be."

She slumped down onto the edge of the cot. "I'll have no more part of this farce."

"This farce saved you near a decade of hard labour. Now I can haul you off to the outback, have you break stone from sunrise to sunset if you'd prefer, or I can take you home. You can see your daughter and attend a party as the guest of honour."

Mary sat frozen; gaze planted firmly on the floor. In the concrete, visions of her first time riding up the slopes of Faulds Farm appeared before her. The feeling of her head resting against Matthew's shoulder as he guided the reigns, how the fields appeared endless, and the wildflowers that sprouted along the checkered pathways seemed like something out of a fairytale. When their wagon came to a stop out front of the homestead, she had looked down across the fields and thought how lucky she was to get to spend a lifetime here. So much had soured in six short years. *I'd give it all up now, every cent, every acre, just give me Lilith and train tickets to somewhere far away.*

"You listening?" The constable asked as he peeled the door back, "It's hardly much of a choice."

The lawman was right. As much as she despised the town for everything they had done to those she loved, it hardly seemed worth a decade of imprisonment just to prove a point. Those in chains have few options, once released, there would be chances for escape.

"One party, then I'm free? I'm not going to be dragged back here afterwards?"

"Not by me. He gave you a full pardon, once I deliver you home our business is done."

Mary got to her feet and the constable led her out of the station. The blinding light of the morning sun stung her eyes and forced her to a squint. Sweat soaked her forehead. Her skin turned red, and her hands grew tight and swollen. She had not been outdoors in days, and she was being punished for it.

Beside the station a large brown Appaloosa, frosted along its back with white hair stood tied to a small wood railing. Dunne helped boost her into the saddle, mounting with one arm proved difficult and it took three attempts before she managed to stay on. "So, what is this celebration for exactly?" Mary asked, "A party for digging a hole? Doesn't seem like a can't miss event."

The constable leapt up in front of her, "Don't know," he said with a slight pant in his breath, "He wanted a party so there's a party. The good priest said something about a ceremony too, but that's all they'll tell me. It's been all secrets since you shot Mackenzie, reckon your little one is the only one who really knows what's going on."

Bowdern's the only one, Mary might have said.

"Yahl's being run by a girl who can't count to ten without her fingers and this makes sense to you?"

"Hard to argue with gold, and your daughter's got a lot of it."

"Promised a lot of it," Mary corrected.

As they rode, Mary started noticing magpies perched and watching all along their route. Atop every street sign and fence post, scattered amongst the trees. There were no caws, no flutter of wings. They sat as still as statues, only their dirty red eyes moved. "Do you see them watching us?" Mary asked.

The constable scoffed, "Usually takes longer in lock up for someone to get this paranoid."

"I'm not paranoid."

You are, it's all in your head. Father Dirt has made you crazy.

As they left the town proper and places to perch grew scarcer, so did the birds. *All in your head.* A tentative calm returned to her and with it some hope. *Perhaps not all is lost, too late to save the farm from the town, but not too late to escape the town.*

Mounting the Appaloosa was proof enough that she could not ride, but she could walk, and struggle as she might, one arm was enough to carry Lilith. A plan took shape in Mary's mind. In the evening, when the town was good and drunk from the party she would slip away with her daughter and whatever she could stuff into a suitcase. If they left before midnight, they could make it to Mount Gambier by sunrise and catch the early train to Adelaide. City life would be hard, but they would be safe, and Lilith could go back to being a child rather than a prophet. It would be a long and difficult night, but it was the only option, they had already stayed in Yahl too long.

At the approach of Faulds Farm the constable dismounted, opened the front gate, and led the horse up the slope by its reins. Over in the outer paddock the whole town had gathered, Mary could not make out any faces from the distance, but by the sounds of laughter and jovial chatter she could tell everyone was in good spirits.

Large tent poles connected by strings of brightly coloured flags circled The Pile and the hole. Food and drink were being served from the backs of wagons, the breeze rich with the smell of lemon tarts, cinnamoned apples, plum scones, and meat pies. The last of the weeds had been cut away, and families picnicked all around. Children climbed the small dirt piles that surrounded the hole and fair games played out along the field's edges. Dunne and Mary continued up to the homestead.

A welcoming party awaited them on the veranda. Alice Williams stood by the door, beside her Miss Mackenzie sat on a kitchen chair, a walking stick resting over her lap. Behind the spinster were two sheepish looking girls, both no older than thirteen, faces Mary had not seen before. All four were dressed in matching white dresses.

The constable halted the horse and lowered Mary down. Her feet had barely touched the ground before Alice was upon her. "Mary," she cried, "It's so good to have you back."

"Where's Lilith? I want to see my daughter."

The spinster rose to her feet. Wobbling as she went, the two girls by her side rushed to brace her until she found her footing beneath the walking stick. "She's up at The Pile," said the old bag through a smug grin, "Speaking with her father."

Even with a dress covering her leg Mary could see the wads of lumpy bandages wrapped around the spinster's knee and thigh. *At least I got her as good as Tom got me.*

Mary turned her back to the women; she managed only a few steps before Dunne blocked her way. Alice saddled up beside her and linked their arms together, "There'll be plenty of time for that. We must get you ready for the festivities first."

Alice led her up towards the homestead. "I'm fine as I am," said Mary.

"Some women take no pride in their appearance," mumbled Mackenzie to her attendants.

"And some have nothing to take pride in!"

The girls giggled quietly to themselves. Mary expected the old woman to be angry or upset, but she simply shook her head and smiled. It was a wide toothy smile that scrunched her face and brought out all her wrinkles. "See you out there dear."

The spinster limped away, a girl at each side, helping her keep balance as she moved off towards The Pile.

"Come now," said Alice, dragging Mary inside, "We spent a good long while sewing your dress for today, it would be awful to let that work go to waste."

As she was led up through the homestead Mary was taken aback by how clean the house was, she always kept a tidy home, but nothing like this. The floorboards and stairs had been polished to a shine, walls repainted, furniture re-stained, and the smell of baked goods and ripe fruit drifted in from the kitchen.

She was taken to her bedroom. From behind the closed-door she heard friendly chatter and smelt the strong scent of lavender perfume. When the door opened the conversation stopped and eight of Yahl's young women stood staring at her. Each donned a floor length white dress, pale powder make-up, and wore their hair neatly curled in a low hanging bun. Quaint smiles adorned each of their faces. None looked her in the eyes.

Mary felt uneasy at the sight of them. They were like copies of one another, some slightly taller or shorter, others curvier or thinner, but all eerily alike. "What's going on?" She asked.

Alice unlocked their arms and placed a hand on Mary's back, "Come now," she said, not answering Mary's question.

Alice guided her to the back corner of the room where a small bronze bathtub had been placed, flower petals topped the water and thin wispy strands of steam rose up into the air.

"We're here to help, now, let's get you cleaned up."

"I'm not bathing for an audience," said Mary.

Alice clapped her hands twice in quick succession and the girls all turned their backs to the tub. "No one will peek," said Alice, "I promise."

Mary had been subjected to an array of strangeness the past month but even still this felt odd to her. Her stomach twisted to knots, and she found herself gripped by an uneasiness she was unable to put to words. *They've all gone mad.*

Intuition told her to refuse the bath, to refuse it all, push Alice aside and make a break for the bush. The women weren't dressed for a chase, if she made it out the backdoor, she'd have a couple hundred yards on any serious pursuers, not to mention the element of surprise. A throbbing in her elbow brought her to a hunch and stopped her before she had any real chance to consider escape. She was malnourished, with only one good arm, a couple hundred yards was not enough of a head start. *Mother always said patience was a virtue, wait for the cover of night, wait until you have Lilith.*

She looked to the crystal-clear water in the tub, then to herself. Her dress had turned to rags, stained, torn, and stiff against her underarms with dried sweat. Her skin itched from days old layers of dirt that had not been properly washed. Her fingernails were gnawed and embedded with grime. Between her legs was red and raw with rash and blood. A bath had never been more tempting, and she found herself unable to resist.

The wife Williams turned her back and Mary removed her makeshift sling and clothing. As quickly and quietly as she could she pulled the days old rag from her undergarments, wrapped it up in her dress and stuffed it underneath a nearby dresser. Looking about it appeared that the women had stayed true to their word, and none had seen what she had done. Mary sighed, relieved.

Stepping into the bath had her feeling like a woman beyond her years, it was not just her elbow that was broken, it was her spirit too. The cell had weakened her, the days of unbroken pain even more so. She was hunched and moved like a newborn foal; awkward and uncertain.

The water was divine, and as she slowly lowered herself down into it, the blood and dirt that soiled her skin drifted away effortlessly. She submerged her head beneath the water, a second baptism. Had it not been for Lilith she could've stayed in the bath for days, but Mary wanted to see her daughter and she wanted to see her now.

Pulling herself to her feet, she stepped out onto the hardwood, leaving behind a tub of muddy water. None of the women turned to face her, but two moved to her dresser, one retrieved a towel, the other a robe. Mary dried her body and wrapped herself in the robe. All at once the girls turned to face her. They moved in perfect unity, as though they shared a single mind.

"Feeling better?" Alice asked.

"I'll feel better once I'm allowed to see Lilith."

"There'll be plenty of time for all that later."

Alice gestured to one of the girls and they left the room, a few moments later they returned with a doctor in tow, a stout bald man in a white coat. He provided her with a morphine injection and applied a proper sling to her arm before promptly leaving. The doctor never spoke a word and never looked her in the eyes. Everything he did was explained by Alice.

The morphine left her tired and nauseous, but it was worth it to be rid of the pain. With her bathed and medicated, the young handmaidens got to work. They each performed a duty, all in service to her. Some rubbed lotions and tonics into her arms and legs, some curled and styled her hair, others applied subtle make up and doused her in perfume. At first it felt overwhelming and claustrophobic, but once she got used to the chaos of being doted on by so many, she found the experience strangely pleasurable.

Mary could not say how long they spent readying her, the girls never stopped working but were cautious to take their time.

"It starts when we say," said Alice, "No oversights, you must be flawless."

She sounds like mother. When all was finally done, they presented her with a hand mirror. She could hardly believe she was looking at a reflection, not since her wedding day had she seen herself look so perfect. Even with all the stress and hardship she had endured, she was still beautiful.

Next came the dress, one of the handmaids fetched it from the wardrobe and presented it to her. It was breathtaking. An elegant gown made of ivory silk and satin, with puffed sleeves, a sinched waist and a light flowing skirt embroidered with waves of beaded pearls. *Of course it had to be white,* Mary thought, *Still, this is marvellous, they should hate me, but instead they treat me like royalty.*

Suspicion faded once they placed her in the dress, it fit better than she could have imagined. She had never looked so glamourous and likely never would again. *Queen of the country today, homeless in the city tomorrow.*

Heels as white and pristine as marble followed, then a necklace of silver with a pendant of amethyst, and earrings of polished opal. It was all stunning, but none of the finery was as cherished as the folded scrap of menstrual cloth that one of the older handmaidens discreetly gave her. With the fear of ruining the dress lessened, she enjoyed the fashion for the fleeting moments allowed. They'd no sooner put her in the gown when Alice told them, "It's time to go."

"Where?" Mary asked, "Are you taking me to see Lilith now?"

"We are, I think we've kept them all waiting long enough."

Taking up bouquets of white roses, Alice and the girls lined up around her. Alice led the way, two stayed at Mary's side and the rest paired off and followed behind. Moving down through the homestead Mary found herself reminiscing about her time spent at Faulds Farm. Once the party was underway, she would need to take whatever chance she could to escape, more likely than not there would be no chance to make it back inside before running. *This may be the last time I set foot in our home.*

At first, she thought of Matthew, of their first night together, running around the sitting room, sipping on whiskey and singing folk tunes, but as the front door drew closer, her mind turned to Lilith. To the agony of her birth and the joy of holding her in her arms for the first time. The feeling of seeing her take her first steps. The shudder when she fell trying to climb the bannisters. Early mornings baking scones and biscuits, late nights by candlelight reading ghost stories. *She's always loved a good scare.* The front door swung open, and the procession stepped out into the dry summers air. Home and the past were gone, and there was no getting them back.

They moved down the front yard slope. Dust kicked up all around them as they walked and clung to the hems of their dresses. None of the women appeared concerned. Each wore half a years wages in fabric and labour, yet none fussed at the destruction of it. *They really must think Matthew has riches waiting for them, the fools.*

The breeze carried the wails of a harmonica intermingled with laughter and merry chatter in from the fields. Mary glanced over to the outer paddock where the party was already underway. The sun was harsh in her eyes, and all she could see were shadows. Blotchy shapes of men, women, and children, each of whom played, ate, and drank beneath The Pile.

She could see no faces but as they moved further down the trail, she felt their eyes on her. The shadows slowed, the laughter dissipated, the chatter fell to a whisper. The harmonica shrieked to a halt and everyone along with it. No one moved. No one spoke. Everyone stared.

Mary found herself scratching at the back of her wrist as her walk slowed. The two women following behind forced her back to pace. "Stop that," one of them whispered, "You'll ruin yourself for him."

Mary tried to stop but couldn't, she had not felt this nervous since walking down the aisle at her wedding. There had been a happy ending waiting at the end of that walk, she did not expect the same to be true this time.

She wished she had listened to George sooner, fought Father Dirt harder. *I underestimated Lilith,* Mary thought, *Overestimated the town. I thought there was more sense, more respect... God I wish I was smarter; I could've done something. None of this had to happen.*

As the procession reached the outer paddock gate Mary finally saw the town clearly. Everyone wore white, man and woman, young and old, but Mary paid little mind to their clothes. She was fixated on the sea of watchful faces, a sea of faces stained with streaks of crusted mud.

Each set of glaring eyes framed by black and brown grime. Some had drawn patterns and symbols on their cheeks and foreheads, others had just smeared the dirt across themselves, but no face was clean.

The mass of hundreds stood huddled shoulder to shoulder around the freshly dug hole. A dozen small mounds jutted up throughout the crowd, each one topped by a burly man with a shovel, standing at attention like a soldier on guard. Big Tom manned one such pile. His face dirtied by three shoddily drawn crosses atop his brow and streaks like claw marks down the length of his cheeks. Dirt aside it was the nicest Mary had ever seen the man look. Clean shaven, clothes tucked and pressed. The change unnerved her. She looked into his eyes and saw nothing; the kindness had faded from him.

Alice and the handmaidens led her into the crowd. Mary put on a brave face, but she could not hide the panic in her breathing, and she could not stop herself from picking at the back of her hand. She slouched down and kept her head low, trying to avoid eye contact as much as spot her daughter. Amongst them were dozens of dirty children with unkempt hair, but none were hers.

At the edge of the hole a space had been left for her between Father Bowdern and Miss Mackenzie. The priest was dressed in his finest vestments, a robe of while lace and silk, embroidered with repeating patterns of the Star of Bethlehem. A blood red cape was fastened around his sagging neck, the same colour as the bible he clasped against his chest. A small fleck of brown stained his forehead.

Mary was placed between the two seniors, only then did some of the eyes on her look away. Alice and her attendants left her, walked up to The Pile, took up handfuls of dirt and smeared it across their faces. Mary's stomach tightened, everyone else was already dirtied but seeing the young women applying the muck to themselves after spending so long making themselves up was deeply unnerving. *Focus on your breathing. Find Lilith. Run.*

A cold wrinkled hand came down on her shoulder, "Relax my dear," said Father Bowdern, "Everything is as it should be."

"Where's my daughter?"

"Where she belongs," interrupted Mackenzie, her voice shrill and piercing, like nails down a chalkboard, "At her father's side."

Hidden amongst the crumbling peak of The Pile Mary spotted her daughter. It was no easy task. While the town had painted their faces in grime, Lilith had covered her entire body, and without a keen eye she was easily lost to the dirt. She had become part of The Pile.

From the ground Mary could not even tell if the girl was clothed, so much of her had been consumed by filth. Her hair looked like a cow pie, crusted and clumped together in a solid piece. Merely imagining the stench of it caused Mary's throat to tighten.

"Lilith," she shouted, "Come down to Mumma, please!"

"Quiet," hissed Mackenzie.

"There's no need for that," said Father Bowdern, "Stay silent child. Now that you are here, we can begin."

"Begin what?"

The priest offered no answer, only a raised finger to his lips. He cleared his throat and began addressing the town, "Brothers! Sisters! We stand here today on the precipice of a golden age for our small town."

The old man started shuffling about the edge of the hole, looking into the eyes of his parish as he spoke, "After today, thanks to the glory of God and the kindness of our departed brethren Father Dirt, we shall be lifted up. Yahl will be transformed into the new Garden of Eden!"

The priest raised up a handful of dirt from one of the small mounds circling the hole and gestured with it as he continued round the pit, "No longer will we need to toil, no longer will we need to suffer. Through Father Dirt we will hear the word of God and live holy lives without worry. Last night our angel atop The Pile spoke to the good father and he told her, along with myself and dear Miss Mackenzie what must be done. Now she shall speak with him again for us all to see and we will do as Father Dirt bids, for he is our salvation... Remember, no glory was ever gained without sacrifice."

Even now when she had been so thoroughly bested Mary felt compelled to speak up for Matthew's memory, "This is nonsense," she cried, "This—"

Two small hands smothered her mouth and took her words from her, it was Mackenzie's girls.

"This is God's work!" Shouted Father Bowdern, "And there shall be no more interruptions."

The priest returned to Mary's side and raised both hands up towards The Pile, "Speak to us my child, give us the Father's word."

"Praise the Father!" Shouted an unseen man.

"Bless us Father Dirt!" Cried a woman.

Lilith raised her hands. Everyone and everything went still. All eyes were on the little girl.

There was tension in the air. A collective anxiety. Mary shared their feelings but not their reasons. They awaited wealth, she anticipated more pain, and more blasphemy against her departed. When her child finally spoke, gasps and cheers erupted from the crowd in equal measure.

"Father Dirt says," yelled Lilith, "Father Dirt says thank you for all your hard work. He has lots of gold for you all, and good weather and good fortune too. He just wants one thing in return first."

"Anything!" A man shouted.

"Bless you Father Dirt!" Shrieked another.

Mary felt her little girl's eyes fall onto her. Lilith had always seemed to avoid looking her way when she preached her nonsense, but now she stared.

"Father Dirt says..." Continued Lilith.

There was hesitation in her voice. She broke her gaze with Mary and started looking about the crowd. "He..."

"Tell us!" Screamed one of the handmaids.

"Speak child," demanded Mackenzie, "Do not waver now."

"Father Dirt says!" Lilith shouted, "Father Dirt says he misses his wife."

All at once the town's eyes were back on Mary.

"He misses his wife, and he wants her back. Mumma and father will be together forever in the dirt."

There were no cheers or shouts, only mumbled questions. Half the crowd shared Mary's confusion, the rest watched on with cold indifference, faces as unflinching as statues. "No," Mary said, her voice riddled with panic, "No, no. Lilith?"

Lilith said nothing. Mackenzie smiled. Father Bowdern leaned in close, "I warned you Father Dirt had his limits."

The old man stepped back, raised both his hands to the heavens and shouted for all to hear, "Honour thy father, place her in the hole!"

With rope and bindings in hand, the spinster's inner circle were the first to move. "Accept your blessing," one of them snarled as they edged towards her.

"You can't do this!" Mary insisted, "It's all lies, there's no Father Dirt, it's Bowdern, Mackenzie!"

Her words fell on deaf ears. The crowd closed in around her. Mary kicked off a shoe and with her good arm raised it up and started swinging it about. "Lilith!" She shrieked, "Tell them to stop! Tell them to stop please!"

"Show some dignity before your husband," said Father Bowdern.

"Grab her already," barked Mackenzie.

A young man with a pockmarked face obeyed his master and rushed at her. With all the strength she could muster Mary swung at him. The heel caught the man in the eye, ripping through his pupil until a sickening pop brought red tears.

The man screamed and Mary screamed back. She yanked the shoe free, and a spray of blood and viscera shot across her face. The man fell to his knees with both hands pressed against his face, desperately trying to keep what little remained of his eyeball in its socket. He sobbed and cried out for his mother. For God. For Father Dirt. For anyone to help. But no one moved.

Mary was trembling. She held the heel high, ready to strike again. It was far from the begging man's face now, but she could still feel his eye squishing just beyond her grip. It made her want to throw up. "Leave me be," she managed to shout, "This is madness."

"This is God's work," cried Miss Mackenzie, "Now are you lot men or dogs?"

Only one proved himself a man in the spinster's eye, the one Mary dreaded the most. Big Tom thrust the blade of his shovel into the dirt mound where he stood and with long arched strides stepped down into the mob. Like the Red Sea the mass parted to let him through.

He had never looked so strong, so menacing. "Ain't no need for violence," he said.

Mary feigned a lunge at him, shaking the bloodied heel like a hatchet. The big man did not flinch. "Please Tom, don't let them do this. I'm your friend, Matthew was your best friend, he would want you to help us."

"I am," said the big man, "This is what he wants, he just said so."

"A child's words," said Mary, "Matthew hasn't spoken once, only Lilith."

"She speaks with her father's voice," called the spinster.

"Shut up! Lies, lies, lies, murder for a confused little girl."

Big Tom shook his head, "Ain't that way Mary. I was at the wedding, youse both said you'd be together forever, now's the time."

"Bastard," Mary said coldly, "You'd be dead in a ditch by now if it wasn't for me and Matthew. This is how you repay us?"

For a heartbeat, the distant look in his eyes faltered and Mary saw her friend again. If she had more time there may have been a chance to sway the old farmhand, but the crowd was growing uneasy, and Mackenzie's patience was running short. "On with it," The hag demanded.

The big man winced, as if what he was about to do would hurt him as much as it hurt her. He charged and Mary swiped at him. The heel grazed his cheek, leaving behind a pale scratch of pulled up skin. It looked painful but did nothing to slow or stop him.

The giant flung himself around her, wrapping her in a tight bearhug. She kicked wildly as he raised her up off the ground. "Yield," he ordered in a gruff whisper; Mary refused.

His thick arms tensed and tightened around her. All the good of the morphine vanished in an instant as her elbow pressed in against her ribs. She braced for more snaps or pops, more broken bones, but none came. Still there was pain, as sharp and fresh as when the joint was first broken. It felt as though her ribcage and organs were shifting inside of her, flattening. Finally, she screamed and dropped the shoe, and the hold eased slightly.

She thrashed and cursed, but there was nothing to be done. Around her the town started to move and speak once again, but Mary's voice rose above them all, "Lilith, I beg you please!"

There was no answer from above. Father Bowdern stepped forward and with a clammy hand brushed a lose lock of hair behind Mary's ear, "Don't fuss now," he said, "Go to your husband with dignity."

Mary spat in the old man's face. The frothed clump of saliva struck him between the eyes and left him looking like a rabbit at the end of a shotgun. "Get used to it," Mary snarled, "I'll spit down on you in Hell every chance I get!"

The priest wiped away the spit with his sleeve, "Restraints," he barked, "Enough fussing about. Father Dirt wants his bride."

Mackenzie's fanatics began looping rope around her, binding her wrist and lashing her arms against her sides. *There'll be no escape once they're done.* "It's them!" Mary shouted, unsure exactly who she meant her words for, "Bowdern, Mackenzie, they tricked my little girl for their own ends. A storm and some gold that barely anyone has seen, it's all a lie, Father Dirt's a lie. They want me dead so I can't prove it."

She reared her head back and looked Tom in the eye as best she could, "He threatened me at the bonfire, me and George. Our priest poisoned your friend I know it. Matthew would never do this, Matthew would never want this!"

"But Father Dirt does," said the spinster.

"An unbeliever and a lunatic share the same mind," added Father Bowdern, "We must try and forgive her and pay no mind to the horrid lies she speaks."

The crowd let out murmurs of approval. "Ain't no need to be scared now," said Tom, "You're going to a better place."

Breathes came fast and shallow, and Mary's heart pounded so violently against her chest she thought it might burst.

"Mercy!" She screamed, as tears rushed down her cheeks, "I beg you all, mercy! You can have it, Faulds Farm, Lilith too. I won't stand in your way anymore I swear. She can live out on the dirt if that will make you all happy, just please show mercy!"

"We can't go against Father Dirt's wishes," said Mackenzie as she limped forward towards Mary, "But don't worry, I'll take good care of Lilith while you're away with your husband."

Mary screamed again. She swung a free leg and kicked the cane out from underneath the spinster. The old woman slammed into the ground like a dropped sack of manure, squealing like a feral pig as she hit the dirt and rolling about like one too.

One of the spinster's cronies struck Mary across the face for the attack. She tried to get them back, but the ropes and Big Tom kept her from getting even.

The two young servant girls helped the old bag to her feet. "Put her in," Mackenzie demanded, "Throw her if you have to."

Hastily, Mary's ankles were bound, and she was dragged to the edge of the hole. Looking down into the empty abyss, she was forced to accept the truth, there would be no escape. *There are worse places to die,* she told herself, *But no worse way.* Tears streamed down her cheeks, washing away the young man's blood that covered her face and spreading it down to her dress. She had not wept so uncontrollably since her first night alone without Matthew.

Additional ropes were fastened around her bindings and pulled tight. "From the Earth we are blessed," cried Father Bowdern, "And to the Earth we must return."

The crowd surged up around her. "Father Dirt! Father Dirt! Father Dirt!"

A shove in the back from a face she did not see pushed her over the edge and into the hole. A scream erupted from her, but was quickly silenced, as the bindings tugged back against her chest, knocking the wind from her. Barely a foot deep, the ropes had caught her. Slowly she was lowered into the darkness, "Lilith!" She shouted, "Please, I love you."

At long last her daughter acknowledged her, "Relax wombat, everything works out in the end!"

She sank deeper and deeper into the ground. Above the faces of her community hung over her, leering and watching with morbid curiosity as she was placed into her grave, alive and well. The grave was far deeper than what George had been laid to rest in. Twenty feet, if not more, Mary guessed. *It's done now. Even with two good arms and no restraints, there's no chance of me climbing out of this.*

A shiver ran up her spine as she hit the bottom, the dirt was cold and filled with jagged chunks of broken rock. Above her the faces slipped away, until all that remained were the dozen large men who'd topped the smaller mounds surrounding the grave. They held their shovels in hand, trowels filled with soil. "Father Dirt!" Lilith shouted, her voice faint and high pitched.

Hundreds echoed the call and cried out for the false prophet, "Father Dirt! Father Dirt! Father Dirt!"

The spades upended and dirt rained down. Each cluster that fell hit her like a punch. One struck her stomach with such force that she tasted vomit. She twisted and squirmed, trying her best to avoid the falling dirt, to get to her feet. It was a fool's task. Her bindings were too tight, and the dirt fell too fast and too heavy. Anytime she raised herself even slightly, a fresh wave of grime came crashing down and forced her back into submission.

Overhead the shovels continued to swing back and forth as she struggled. Some of the digger's smiled at her, others looked saddened, but all filled the grave, even Tom.

"I'll give you anything!" Mary shouted, "Anything, please!"

Her pleas were drowned out by the chants, "Father Dirt! Father Dirt! Father Dirt!"

All Mary could do was wait as the earth rose around her. In no time her lower half was almost fully covered and at her sides the soil touched her ears. With each shovel of dirt her chest grew tighter. Breathes shallower. Clumps of soil blocked her nose and stuck to the back of her throat like balls of phlegm that could not be coughed up. Her skin turned blotchy and red with irritation. She itched all over. Itched in places she never would have imagined.

A tickle moved up her thighs. Shaking what dirt she could from her legs she strained her neck up to see. Worms and millipedes, scurrying amongst the soil, writhing, and slithering up and down her body. *They'll be feasting on my skin come nightfall.* She burst out in laughter at the thought, just as a trowel of black dirt struck her face. Coughing and choking on the earth, the cackling did not stop.

She gave up fighting her restraints. Gave up resisting. She rocked back and forth in the filth, howling out a deep, uncontrollable belly laugh. Father Dirt's name died out and the shovelling stopped as curious faces leaned over the edge of her abyss.

"You're all doomed," she cackled, "It's Hell or me, either way, this whole town will suffer!"

There was murmuring above, then the shovelling resumed. No one called for Father Dirt. The farm was silent, but for the faint hiss of spades ripping into earth.

"I go to God laughing, you'll go to Hell screaming!"

More and more dirt consumed her, soon nothing but her face remained uncovered. The weight was unbearable. Her bones and organs compressed. Each breath hurt, and finally, the laughter stopped. She could not move, only lay and wait. There was panic, but not from fear, rather anticipation. *It's alright,* she told herself, *I'll be with Matthew soon. Not in the ground, but in the Heavens.*

Dirt piled up over her face, stinging her eyes and covering the last of her. Above the town disappeared, replaced with darkness. Voices faded to nothing. All that remained was the thumping of fresh earth as it fell atop her. Each breath she drew was shallower than the last and came filled with more and more dirt, until dirt was all there was. *Matthew?*

About the Author

Taylor J. Thompson is an Australian horror and weird fiction author. A lover of punk rock, football, and rum. He currently resides in Australia with his partner and their two cats.

You can find him on Instagram/Threads *@taylorjthompsonauthor.*
Read more at https://substack.com/@taylorjthompson.

www.ingramcontent.com/pod-product-compliance
Lightning Source LLC
Chambersburg PA
CBHW022022170626
46808CB00003B/1020